Beat the Drum Slowly

Drifter Blake Durant was arrested and thrown into the Sunfish Creek jail on a simple case of mistaken identity. The town was expecting a visit from outlaw Tom Moran, who'd sworn to get revenge on its lawmen, and Deputy Billy Owen suspected that Blake was part of Moran's gang, sent out ahead of the main gang to scout the lay of the land.

Then everything became even more complicated when some genuine owlhoots broke jail and committed a cold-blooded murder. A manhunt followed, as did the unexpected appearance of Moran's beautiful young daughter, Lisa. And Blake found himself on the trail of the outlaws . . . because the only way to clear himself of the murder was to bring back the guilty parties, either in their saddles . . . or across them.

Beat the Drum Slowly

Sheldon B. Cole

A Black Horse Western

ROBERT HALE

First published by Cleveland Publishing Co. Pty Ltd,
New South Wales, Australia
First published in 1967

© 2019 by Piccadilly Publishing

This edition © The Crowood Press, 2020

ISBN 978-0-7198-3116-4

The Crowood Press
The Stable Block
Crowood Lane
Ramsbury
Marlborough
Wiltshire SN8 2HR

www.bhwesterns.com

Robert Hale is an imprint
of The Crowood Press

Typeset by Derek Doyle & Associates, Shaw Heath
Printed and bound in Great Britain by
4Bind Ltd, Stevenage, SG1 2XT

ONE

SUNFISH CREEK

Blake Durant came to a halt at the base of a rust-colored butte. Its meager shade offered little relief from the heat, but merely to be out of the glare of the sun after many hours in the saddle seemed as refreshing as a swim in a clear spring. Durant's mouth was parched and his skin was tight, his cheeks temporarily pock-marked by the day's wind-whipped grit.

Unsaddling Sundown, his powerful black stallion, Blake Durant let the horse pick at the poor grass on the rocky slope. He made a fire and boiled coffee, then sat on a ledge of rock, leaning forward, elbows on his knees, and studied the harsh country before him. The coffee helped to take some of the heat out of his sun-scorched body, but he knew he was in for an uncomfortable night under the blanket of heat which lay around him. It had been the same for five days and nights of riding aimlessly, on no definite trail, trying to forget what he'd left behind and disinterested in what lay ahead. To Blake Durant, little had mattered for several years spent riding from one end of the country to the other, searching for he knew not what, continuing on only because the past had to be buried, had to be forgotten.

He finished the coffee and hobbled Sundown so the big black wouldn't stray, then he stretched out on his blanket. He laid his hide coat on a shoulder of rock and put his gunbelt on top of it. His boots he placed at the bottom of the rock. Ready for the night now, he lay there, the heat pressing down on him. He closed his eyes, blanked out his mind, and fell off to sleep.

He was in the saddle pressing on before the first gray light of another summer day pushed back the night. With the sun behind him an hour later, he topped a rise and saw a small town ahead, a huddle of buildings on the banks of a creek. At that early hour there was no activity that he could see. He rode towards the town without enthusiasm, expecting nothing from it and unwilling to give anything of himself in return. The one gratifying thing about the place being there at all was the fact that for a short time he'd be able to get some comfort for himself and some rest and feed for Sundown.

Riding into the one street, he slowed the big black. Deep shadows filled the street, making the store section on his right a vague blur of shapes. All doors were closed and there was no sound. Blake stopped, suddenly aware that the silence was too complete. Even at that early hour, somebody should be moving about – a cleaner, a cowhand making an early start for home after a night's recklessness, a townsman wanting to get a jump on competing businessmen, even a crying child. But the street was completely empty and there was no sound but the low moan of the wind.

Somewhere behind him a door hinge creaked. Blake felt his shoulders tighten, but he didn't bother to turn in the gray to check. Sundown stomped impatiently when Blake reined up in the middle of the street. Blake spoke quietly until the big black calmed. Then a voice sounded:

'First thing you do, stranger, is unhook that gunbelt and let it drop. Don't make no fast moves now . . . be real slow and easy like and maybe there won't be trouble.'

Blake was tempted to turn then but he didn't. He hooked the reins about the pommel of the saddle and asked, 'Why?'

'No matter why. Just do like you're told.'

There was a definite ring of authority in the deep voice. Blake calculated that the man was no more than twenty feet behind him. That would put him in the doorway of the slab-fronted building he had just passed. He unbuckled his gunbelt and let it slide from his lean waist. It fell to the street near Sundown's hind legs.

Behind Blake, gravel crunched and then a shadowy movement caught his attention. He turned his head and looked into the upraised face of a man who'd stooped to pick up the gunbelt. When the man's hand closed around the leather, a spark of satisfaction came into wide-set blue eyes. Then the man stepped away, tossing the gunbelt across his shoulder and making a gesture with his gun for Blake to climb down. Blake slipped off Sundown and pulled the big black close to him. The black nuzzled at his shoulder. Blake raised a hand and ran it across the horse's head.

The man with the gun had retreated to the boardwalk. He held the gun on Blake, his face tight and wary. 'Billy, come and take this.' He held Blake's gunbelt behind him, the butt of the big Colt resting on the warped boards.

A younger man, tow-haired, came through the doorway of the building. He took the gunbelt and studied Blake Durant carefully.

Blake said, 'What the hell is this all about?'

'Billy, take his horse and tether it out back. You, mister, come inside and answer some questions. If you've got the right answers, you'll get an apology and your horse and gun back, no harm done. If you ain't got the right answers, it'll be too bad – for you.'

Blake held the man's gaze easily. A mistake had been made by these men, and this fact would soon be realized. In the meantime there was no sense trying to buck them. He let the younger man lead Sundown down a side alley and then he crossed to the boardwalk. The man with the gun shifted quickly aside; then, as Blake entered the room beyond the door, he came up fast behind him. Passing Blake, but still keeping his big gun trained on him, the heavily built man crossed to a desk littered with papers held down by two coffee cups and a black coffee pot. The man slid behind the desk, opened a drawer and pulled out a tin star that he pinned to his shirt.

'The name's Blake Durant, Sheriff,' Blake said. 'Whoever it is you're looking for it's not me.'

'Who I'm lookin' for, mister, I don't rightly know,' the sheriff answered tightly. 'Sit down.'

Blake pulled a chair from the wall, turned it around and straddled it. The back door behind the big man opened and the younger man, Billy, entered. He looked puzzled about something.

The sheriff said, 'Well?'

Billy shook his head. 'Nothing in his saddle-bags to say who he is. Provisions, eating utensils, some tobacco, a silk scarf. Saddleroll didn't help none either.'

The sheriff held out his hand for Blake's gunbelt and then Billy went on, 'Far as I can make out, the gun ain't been fired for some time. Been looked after though; it's as clean as a whistle. And the holster has been oiled. It's real gun-handler gear.'

Blake held the younger man's stare evenly. It was becoming clear to him that trouble in these parts had made these two suspicious of every stranger who rode through. In that case he had no worries if he got a chance to explain himself. The sheriff hooked the gunbelt on a wall peg and sat back in his chair while Billy positioned himself to Blake's right where he could intercept any move towards the back or front doors. Billy's stare stayed on Blake . . . expressionless eyes in a dead-sober face.

The sheriff said, 'Okay, Durant, your saddle-bags are clean. Fact is, we don't know a spit more about you now than we did minutes ago when you rode in from the south. So start off tellin' us why you came that way into town, all the way across that hard country at this time of the year, tiring out yourself and your horse. Also tell us what you've been doing with yourself the last month or so.'

Blake studied the lawman intently, seeing the signs of a heavy drinker in the pitted nose. The man was about forty years of age. Although he was heavily built, Blake could see that a lot of the weight had come from easy living. He wasn't a neat man. His clothes were soiled and one side of his shirt collar was askew, caused by a missing button. The tin star had not been pinned on

11

straight. His thick, unruly brown hair was turning gray, and his grayish skin indicated that he seldom went into the harsh sunlight of this area.

Blake got his thoughts in order and was about to detail his recent movements when the sheriff suddenly jerked upright and said:

'Billy, search him. Empty his pockets.'

Billy moved to obey and Blake made no attempt to stop his search. Moments later Billy placed Blake's money and tobacco pouch before the sheriff. The lawman palmed the tobacco pouch aside and fingered the banknotes. While he counted it, his brow rutted.

'Two hundred and seventy-two dollars, Durant. That's a big stake for a man to be carryin' about.'

'No more than most men would have after working four months on a cattle drive, Sheriff. I was away from towns and I'm not one to be wasting my time gambling.'

The sheriff's mouth twisted and he sat back, pushing the money away. 'We'll see about that, Durant. Get on with it.'

'There's little to get on with, Sheriff,' Blake told him, his voice belying the anger beginning to rise within him. 'I worked for Abraham Curlewis down Sorento way for three months, until a few weeks ago. When the drive ended, I decided to look north and see what the prospects were.'

The sheriff gave a grunt which suggested a certain amount of disbelief. 'Never heard of no cattleman named Curlewis, Durant. You, Billy?'

Billy shook his head.

Blake said irritably, 'Check with Sorento then. Curlewis is known for a couple of hundred miles around.'

'No time for checking things like that, Durant. We've got to decide on you within a day or so.' The sheriff leaned forward, his heavy brows crowding his eyes. 'But say we believe you. Why come north from Sorento?'

'Why not?'

'It's damn hard country, mister, the way you came. A smart man would've taken a train and freighted his horse on it, wouldn't he?'

'I didn't know the country was so hard,' Blake said. 'As for my horse, he's bred to take it and he never feels better than when he's on the move, no matter how hard the travelling might be.'

'He'd be about the best horse I've laid eyes on in years, Durant,' said Billy with a sly grin. 'Your rig's real classy, too, like them clothes you're wearin' and that gun of yours. When you put two hundred and seventy-odd dollars alongside all that, it ain't so easy to believe your story about bein' an ordinary cattle hand.'

Blake's look swung to Billy and there was a hint of venom in his dark eyes. But he allowed no anger to show in his face.

'What do you want to believe?' Blake asked.

'That maybe you're an advance man for Tom Moran, Durant. It could be that you use that fancy gun of yours real good and you're here to meet Moran when he comes back today or tomorrow.'

Blake straightened. 'Who the hell's Tom Moran? I've never even heard of the man.'

'Everybody else in these parts has heard of him,' Billy went on, knowing from the sheriff's approving smile that he could have the floor for the moment. 'Tom Moran's a name that puts fear in the heart of every law-abiding citizen in our territory. Tom Moran's a killer, a thief and an animal who we aim to push right to hell out of our territory. We sure don't aim to let him link up with any of his scum friends.'

Blake gave a smile. 'And you think I'm one of his guns, eh?'

'Could be. Most of what I see of you points to

14

you being a liar, Durant, and I reckon that a man who can lie will do just about anything that suits him.' Billy pushed himself away from the wall and looked at the sheriff. 'Lew, I don't reckon we should take any chances with this one. I got a bad feeling in my bones about him. I reckon we should just tumble him into a cell with them others and keep him there. Then, when Moran comes and goes, we can figure what to do with him later.'

Blake got slowly to his feet, his face hard as his gaze moved angrily from the sheriff to the deputy. 'You can both go to hell,' he grated. 'I rode in here minding my own business. I've got no truck with Tom Moran or any of his kind. Just leave me be.'

Billy whipped out his gun and suddenly his face looked older. His eyes were pinched down and Blake saw a streak of meanness in his glare. 'Durant, Tom Moran rode wild through these parts for a long time before we caught up with him and had him jailed. He should've been hanged but somehow he got to the judge and the jury. Our claim that he was the killer of seven men was thrown out of court. But he was convicted on a robbery charge and for the last two years he's been penned up. He got out two days ago, and we have good reason to believe that he'll come storming back here lookin' to get even with Sheriff Cavill. But Tom Moran ain't no fool. No, sir, he ain't the kind to come here alone after two years in prison. He'll get some of his scum crowd to ride along and help him. To do that, to make his contacts, he'd have to go to Willoughby first, which is south of here and right where you came from. He'll contact your kind, send you ahead to prepare things, and then he'll ride in and play hell with the town. We ain't about to let that happen.'

'Look,' Blake said. 'The fact that I rode in from the south and I'm comfortably off for a cattle hand, doesn't mean I'm a gun handler. Do what you like about Moran and his cronies, but leave me out of it. If you don't want me in town, I'll shift on. This town means nothing to me, and what little I've seen of it I don't expect it ever will.'

Billy shook his head. 'No good, Durant. We ain't fools. If you ride off and tell Moran that we're all geared up to cut him down when he comes in, it'll mean we've worked for a week now for nothing.' He shook his head more emphatically and crossed to the desk. He dismissed Blake with a snort and turned to Sheriff Cavill. 'Lew, that's how I see it.'

Cavill rose, nodding grimly. He collected Durant's money and put it in the top drawer of the desk. After he slammed the drawer closed, he let out a deep sigh. 'No trouble now, Durant, and we'll see that you're well fed. This way.'

'Go to hell!' Blake snapped, then Billy's gun dug into his back. Glancing at Billy, Blake saw bitter determination in his eyes. He cursed under his breath and said to Cavill, 'Damn you, mister, when this comes out in my favor, which it will finally, don't expect me to be quiet about it. You're a damned fool.'

'Could be, Durant,' Cavill answered coolly. 'But bein' a fool is a lot better than bein' dead, ain't it? Come on now.'

Cavill walked down a narrow passageway and Blake, prodded by Billy all the way, finally found himself before a cell from which three men looked speculatively at him. Cavill unlocked the cell door, let Blake go in and then he slammed the door shut and locked it.

'Sorry about the crowdin', gents,' Cavill said with a sly grin. 'But this here town ain't used to havin' so many ornery jaspers passin' through.'

17

The sheriff turned away and Billy followed him out. Blake settled back against the bars, looking at each of his cellmates in turn. One was an old-timer, and the other two were rough-looking types who stared back at him with interest. When one of them, a blocky fellow carrying at least a month's stubble on his jaw, asked Blake his name, Blake didn't bother to answer him.

The man didn't pursue the business and Blake sat on one of the two bunks as the three of them looked him over.

TWO

A DEPUTY'S NOTCHES

'Name's Gus Ivers.'

Blake Durant brought his mind back from the memories of the past and looked bleakly at the old man who had just sidled up to him. For five minutes, ever since Cavill and the deputy had left him in the cell, Durant had been moodily regarding the dirty floor, wondering how he could get released. The last six days had taken their toll of his strength and patience. He wanted only to be left alone.

19

'What they got on you, Durant?' the old man asked. 'You caught up in this Moran business, too?'

Blake let his gaze shift past the old man to where the other two were sitting opposite each other playing poker with a grubby old deck of cards. Neither of the pair responded to his look, but Blake had the feeling that their minds were not fully on the card game. He sensed they were listening.

'I'm just passing through,' Blake told the old man.

'Sure, sure, Durant. Don't mind me, son. I'm just looking for some conversation to fill in the time. Them other two ain't said but a couple of words to me all the time we've been penned up together, and what they said was for me to shut up and stay that way.'

Blake studied the old man for a short moment, time enough for him to evaluate the man's age as being something over sixty. He decided that he had lived hard. His clothes were grimy and shapeless on his skinny frame, and his face was deeply lined, weather-pitted and sun-blackened. All his upper teeth were missing, making his cheeks sink against a mouth that was pinched so tight his talk

20

was little more than a grumble of sound as he said:

'I reckon you're different than us, Durant. You got somethin' about you makes me think you ain't no aimless drifter. You in cattle? Mining maybe? Some other business?'

Blake shrugged. 'I'm just drifting.'

Ivers eyed Blake with disbelief. But he muttered, 'That so, eh? Well, there's no tellin', is there? You'd figure a jasper my age, experienced in near every turn of life, could pick a man right, eh? No matter, there's worse things than a drifter.' Ivers threw a sour look towards the other pair. One of them, the shortest, returned his look sullenly. He was solidly built with a thick neck and a lantern jaw. A scar ran down from a corner of his mouth. His small eyes were set close together and almost buried under thick brows.

'Why don't you shut down, Ivers?' he grated. 'I'm sick of listening to you.'

'Too bad, Coolidge,' Ivers answered with an old man's insolence in his voice. 'It's a free world, ain't it? A man's got the right to talk to a friend if he wants, don't he?'

'Friend?' Coolidge snapped. Then he looked at Blake as though seeing him for the first time.

'Yeah, sure, Coolidge. I can tell right off whether a man's friendly or not, and whether I should take the bother to get to know him. But don't you fret none, I ain't gonna be worryin' you on that score. No, sir, not you and not your brother there either. You just mind your own business and I'll mind mine.'

Blake noticed the other man straightening, his hands bending the cards in annoyance. His shoulders squared and for a moment Blake thought he was going to rise and come across the cell to the old man. But then he shifted his feet, stretching out and said, 'Come on, Ed, it's your play. Let the old jasper talk all he likes. The quiet's gettin' on my nerves anyway.'

'To hell with that,' growled Ed, coming to his feet and throwing his cards down on the end of the bunk. He pulled his levis up and cleaned his palms down their front. Then he looked at Blake again and a hint of wariness showed in his eyes before he approached Ivers.

'Leave him be,' Blake said.

Ed Coolidge stopped in mid-stride, a gleam of excitement in his eyes. A nerve jumped in his temple and then his hands went up and became fists.

'You'd be a friend of his then, Durant, just as quick as that, eh?'

'He's done nobody any harm, has he?'

'He's annoyed the belly outa me, mister,' Coolidge said. 'He's been gripin' and whinin' ever since they threw him in here, talkin' big about the old days when he reckoned he was taller'n a pine. I've had my fill of that and I ain't gonna listen to him no more. He's gonna sit quiet or I'm gonna belt his ears back.'

Gus Ivers was on his feet and at Blake's side. He stood there, clearly worried.

'Hold it, Ed.'

The warning came from the other brother, then footsteps sounded along the passageway. Lew Cavill and the deputy arrived a moment later, Cavill frowning and Billy looking pleased. It was Billy who spoke, his voice carrying a mocking lilt:

'You Coolidge boys sure got some imagination. Sure have,' he began. 'Damn me, for a while there you nearly had us believing you were cowhands looking for work, real honest-to-goodness cowmen, bustin' your pants to get behind a herd and eat some dust. Only, like Durant there and old Ivers, you came in on the wrong trail so we just naturally had to check out your story.'

Billy grasped the bars and leaned there, swaying a little from side to side. 'And do you know what we found out?'

Ed Coolidge scowled darkly at Billy while his brother sat, his face hard, his eyes glaring.

'You don't know?' Billy taunted. 'Well, I guess I've just got to surprise you. What we found out was that two jaspers named Ed and Leke Coolidge have for two years now been hellin' it up in and around Willoughby, stealin' and brawlin' and scarin' hell out of folks, till the law there got fed up to the teeth with both of 'em and sent 'em packin'. Only they didn't heed those warnings to shift and they kept comin' back until the sheriff had to throw 'em in a cell. Five times in six months they were jailed and still they couldn't take the hint. And do you know why?'

Ed Coolidge shifted his feet, his face dark and tight. Blake could hear his breath wheezing out.

The deputy chuckled and ran his hands up and down the bars. He held Ed Coolidge's gaze as the big man approached. Lew Cavill looked a little perturbed, but to Blake's surprise he didn't interrupt as his deputy went on:

'I'll tell you why them Coolidge scum stayed on – they had to wait for somebody. They had to be right on hand when Tom Moran, an old trail pard, was let loose from prison. They had to keep their noses clean all that time so they could ride with their old murderin' friend and come back to this town to get revenge for the justice that was handed out.'

Ed Coolidge suddenly lunged forward. He grabbed at Billy's hand but the deputy released the bars and stepped back. Then as Coolidge grasped the bars with both hands, the deputy drew his gun, turned the barrel into his palm and with a growl swung the butt at Coolidge's right hand. The gun butt crushed the fingers of the hand against the bars and Ed Coolidge jumped back, howling in pain and pressing his bloody hand against his chest. His brother charged across the cell but before he reached the barred door, the deputy had his gun trained and ready. Leke stopped, his face purple with hate and rage.

'You're both gonna stay locked up until we figure what to do with you.' Billy's gaze travelled to Blake Durant and his lips peeled back. 'As for you, Durant, we've sent off a message to Sorento to check out your story, but I don't reckon we'll get an answer before Moran gets here. Ivers, you'd like to know maybe that those horses you brought into town across the desert are the property of James Henmore, who'll be coming in later today to file charges against you.'

The deputy holstered his gun as Ed Coolidge moved back to the cell bars, cursing. 'I'm gonna get you, Owen. I'm gonna cut your stinkin' guts out with a rusty knife.'

'With your left hand, Coolidge?' Billy Owen said. Then, easing Sheriff Lew Cavill away, he broke into raucous laughter that filled the passageway and hung in the air even when the sound of the lawmen's footsteps died.

Gus Ivers slumped down on the bunk. Seeing Durant watching him, he muttered sadly, 'Figured Henmore was in the hills and wouldn't be home for a month yet. Damn him, he's always away longer than this.'

Blake Durant put his shoulder to the wall and rested there, knowing that Billy Owen was right about the Coolidge boys being linked with Tom Moran. He could think of a lot of better places to be than in a cell with trouble-making friends of an outlaw plus an old horse thief who should be out buying a porch rocker. But Billy Owen's actions and manner made it clear that Blake would be in the cell for some time yet. He settled down on the end of the bunk, feet up, and watched Leke Coolidge do what he could for his brother's hand. Blake had no sympathy for Ed Coolidge, in fact he felt a measure of relief that Coolidge's injury would keep his mind off troublemaking for a while. Blake Durant closed his eyes and tried to get some sleep.

It was late afternoon and the cell was filled with shadows. Ed and Leke Coolidge had been quiet, keeping to the other end of the cell and talking now and then in low tones. Ivers had slept through noon and was now pacing up and down, looking troubled. Finally he sat beside Blake, glanced at the Coolidge brothers and then he said in a hoarse whisper:

'I reckon you ain't one of 'em, Durant, by the way they don't take to you.'

Blake only grunted. He was fully rested now and impatient to be on the move, and out of this town.

Ivers went on, 'You're what you say you are, and it's a damned pity that Owen don't believe you. Hear me now, Durant – watch him close. He's got a burn in him that makes him right dangerous.'

'He can't hurt me,' Blake said quietly.

'Don't you believe it. That young badge-toter ain't stayin' second-in-charge for long. I been watchin' him real close, ever since he first rode into town about a year ago. He struck people as bein' a real nice, companionable gent. Only that big smile of his ain't true; what's behind it came straight outa hell.'

Blake listened, sensing that Gus Ivers knew what he was talking about this time.

'Take the Petersen business, Durant. Sei Petersen lost a heap of money at Walsh's card table and couldn't afford to. Later, when the saloon closed, Petersen figured to get back some of what he'd been cheated out of, and he waylaid Walsh on his way to his office. Petersen musta hit him pretty hard, I reckon, because Walsh could hardly make himself understood in court the following afternoon with his mouth all busted up. No matter, he had it coming, I reckon. The thing is, Durant, to put you right in the picture, Petersen didn't take more than what he figured was his, and he woulda got clean away and back home if that sneakin' Owen hadn't showed up. Owen said he saw Walsh out cold and bleedin' a treat and he called out to Petersen to stop, but Petersen wasn't havin' any of that, bein' drunk and reckless, and maybe sorry for what he'd done. Petersen made a break for it, Owen says, and drew his gun when Owen called to him a second time.' Gus Ivers leaned closer to Blake, his tobacco-tainted breath making Blake draw away. 'Then Owen said that Petersen shot at him and he was forced to cut him down.'

Ivers straightened, his eyes bright with anger. 'Cut him down,' he repeated hoarsely. 'Three bullets, all in his back.'

Blake frowned at this. He knew there were two versions to each story, and since Deputy Billy Owen wore a badge his story would be the one accepted. But he couldn't see how it was any of his business.

Gus Ivers wasn't finished. Wiping a line of sweat from his brow and licking at his cracked lips, he said, 'And that ain't all, Durant. Reg Petersen, Sei's brother, and Carp, his uncle, rode in to collect the body for burial. They crossed trails with Owen behind the jailhouse and there was a shootout, seen by a lot of folks, in which Owen blasted them both down, killed 'em where they stood. There was no outcry about that either, bein' as it was done in broad daylight. But Owen proved what he was, by hell! – a killer, hiding behind a badge, a damned gunman who don't need much promptin' when it comes to puttin' folks under the sod. You watch him, Durant, because if he don't like you he'll sure enough find some way to push you into an argument. And he's as fast as a blue streak.'

Blake found himself totting up other things he had noticed about Billy Owen. From the very outset Billy Owen had taken charge of things, leaving Sheriff Cavill in the background. It had been the deputy who had examined Blake's possessions and branded him as a gun handler. It had been Owen who had handled the Coolidge boys in the cell before noon, again leaving Cavill in the background. And it had been Owen who had warned Blake that a check was being made on his story. It added up to an ambitious young law officer who was taking full command.

'What about the sheriff?' Blake asked. 'What sort of man is he?'

Ivers shook his head doubtfully. 'Hard to say these days. Once, Lew was a good man, hard but fair. He ran a good, clean town and he could give a little. But since Owen's come, he's changed, slowed right down, got old all of a sudden. I reckon maybe he's scared of Moran coming and figures he won't be able to handle him.'

'But he thinks Owen can?'

'A lot of folk think so. Hell, who else would have worked out that Moran wouldn't come in on his own but would send friends ahead to prepare the way? And who else would have smelled out them Coolidge boys and put 'em where they couldn't do no harm to anybody? I tell you, Durant, Owen's got me scared to my boots. I don't want no part of him, and just as soon as I can talk some sense into Jimmy Henmore about me mistakin' his horses for mine, I'm clearing right out of this territory. Where you headin' after here, Durant? Hell, it don't strike me it would be a hard chore ridin' along with you a ways.'

Blake smiled wryly at the old man, knowing that wherever Gus Ivers went, trouble would follow. 'I haven't made up my mind, Ivers,' he said. 'My worry for now is getting Cavill and Owen to believe my story.'

'Then you got worry enough for the moment, Durant,' Ivers grunted. 'That deputy has got a set against you and I don't reckon any amount of proof is gonna make him change his mind about you. If you get the chance to quit this town, don't stay about playing out your luck. You get and get fast.'

Ed Coolidge stirred from the other bunk. Holding his bandaged fist against his chest, he walked across the cell to the high window. Unable to reach it even on tiptoe, he signaled for his brother to come. Leke worked his hands down his body until he had him about the waist Straining and grunting, Ed finally rose high enough to see out the window. When he came down with a thump, his eyes were bright with excitement. But he immediately sent a withering look at Blake and Ivers before he nudged his brother back into their corner, where he leaned forward, talking too softly for Blake to hear what he was saying.

Shortly after that Leke Coolidge walked to Blake. Shouldering Ivers away, he said tightly, 'Should something happen later tonight, Durant, you and the old-timer keep out of it. If you don't, so help me, there'll come a day when my brother or me, or maybe some friends of ours will hunt you down and shoot your interferin' guts out.'

Ivers moved away, frightened. But Blake coolly returned Coolidge's gaze and gave no reply. Seemingly satisfied, Leke Coolidge returned to his brother's side and gave him a nod as he sat down. From then on, they sat together, watching the passageway that led back to the lawmen's office.

THREE

CORRALLED!

There was no sound in the darkened town. The air in the cell was hot, and each of the four occupants sweated freely. Gus Ivers complained from time to time, but no one took any notice of him. It was, Blake Durant told himself, no time to worry about anything but the escape attempt the Coolidge boys were clearly waiting for. Blake had no way of knowing what Leke Coolidge had seen out there, but he guessed it was a friend. It might even be Tom Moran.

Deep inside Blake was the impulse to call Sheriff Cavill and warn him that something was amiss in his town. Perhaps Cavill, away from Deputy Owens, would accept that Blake was not what Owen claimed, but a loner, a man on the drift. Blake would then be free to go his way. But it was too dangerous to try talking to Cavill. Besides, Blake was no informer.

It was close to midnight when he heard a slight scratching noise outside. Ed Coolidge jumped to his feet and moved quickly to a position under the window.

'Ed?' The voice barely carried through the open, barred window.

'Yeah.'

'Ed, you ready?'

'I been ready twenty hours, damn you. What about the deputy?'

'He's off courtin'. I had to wait. You want the other lawman killed?'

'Do what you have to do.'

Blake Durant shifted on the bunk and dropped his feet to the floor. He peered into the darkness at the two figures pressed against the wall under the high window. He was positive that Sheriff Lew Cavill would soon be dead, but he could see no way of warning the lawman of his fate, unless he shouted out to him. Then he would have both the

Coolidge boys to contend with, but he wasn't really worried on that score.

'Durant, you and Ivers get down on the floor and stay there. We're bustin' out. You keep out of the way and we'll leave the cell door open so you can follow us later. But so help me, don't ruin this, mister, or you're dead.'

Ivers pressed close to Blake, his heart pounding in his sunken chest.

'I'm going, too,' Ivers whispered. 'Owen hates my guts. He'll keep me in here for a month just for borrowin' two damned old ponies.'

Blake pulled Ivers back and pushed him onto the floor, saying, 'Stay put.'

Blake walked across the cell to where Ed and Leke Coolidge stood against the door bars. He said, 'Cavill doesn't have to be killed.'

Ed Coolidge swung about and punched at Blake's face. Blake caught Ed's arm, twisted it hard behind his back and shoved him roughly against the bars. Leke pushed past his brother, driving him harder against the bars, and reached for Blake. Just as his hands seized Blake's throat a shot came from the front of the jailhouse. For a moment Leke Coolidge's grip eased and Blake was able to tear his fingers from his throat. He pounded two blows into Leke Coolidge's stomach and then cracked his elbow into the struggling Ed Coolidge's face. A grunt from Leke was drowned by a howl from Ed.

Then Gus Ivers appeared, clawing his way past all of them as another man worked to open the cell door. Blake heaved Leke Coolidge away as the door opened and Ivers scurried through, ducking under an outflung hand from the man who'd opened the door. Ivers was already running when a second shot broke above the echo of the other one. Blake heard Ivers cry out and then footsteps pounded from the office and died in the street. The man still holding the keys eyed Blake heavily for some time before Leke Coolidge called:

'Stop him, Rudy! Stop the double-crossing scum!'

Blake saw the man's gun lift and he charged. The gun exploded and he felt a burn of pain along his left side. Then his fist struck home, a blow so powerful that it lifted the newcomer off his feet and sent him crashing against the wall. Blake wheeled to see Leke going for the gun which slid across the cell floor. In another moment Leke would have the gun and would use it. So Blake broke into a run, went through the cell door and down the passageway. But before he reached the front door, jumping over the body of Lew Cavill, a figure loomed. Blake had only an instant to recognize Billy Owen, face torn with anger and gun at the ready, then he slammed his shoulder into the powerfully built deputy. Lawman and prisoner went crashing onto the boardwalk, legs and arms entangled. Then Blake jerked his right hand free and drove it down. Owen grunted as blood spurted from his mouth, but he clung desperately to Blake. Blake hit him again and this time Owen's head rocked to the side and his body convulsed under Durant's pinning weight. Blake drew his legs clear of Owen's bulky body and was about to draw back when Owen stirred again, his hands groping. Muttering a curse, Blake knelt and sent two well-timed blows in quick succession onto the point of Owen's jaw. The deputy gave a grunt and his hands dropped to the boards.

Blake rose slowly. From up the street men were coming on the run. There were shouts, then two bullets ripped past Blake's ear. He turned and went back inside. Cavill had dragged himself close to the door, leaving a blood trail on the floor. But then he went still again, seemingly dead.

Getting his gunbelt from the desk, Blake strapped it on as he ran. There was no sense in staying now. If Cavill was dead the town would be in no mood to listen to explanations, and he knew with absolute certainty that Billy Owen would make a claim against him. Then he would hang.

Reaching the jailhouse boardwalk again, Blake risked running the gauntlet of several more shots before he turned into the laneway down which Owen had taken his horse. He was surprised to find Sundown standing quietly, looking out at him from a comfortable stall. Blake's saddle was on the rail. He quickly strapped it on, swung up, and less than a minute after entering the stall he had Sundown running at a gallop.

In the laneway Blake again faced wild shooting and angry shouts. Disregarding them, he pulled Sundown about and raced him for a group of men. They scrambled out of his way as the big black charged. Once through the ring of townsmen, Blake dropped to the neck of the powerful black and clung there. Sundown, without further prompting, stretched out at full gallop.

Ed Coolidge didn't worry where his brother and

Rudy Shelley were as he raced to the three horses. He jumped into the saddle of one and headed towards the western trail out of Sunfish Creek. Although he heard gunfire behind him, he figured it was his duty, first to himself and secondly to Tom Moran, to get away unhurt. If his brother and Shelley didn't make it, too bad.

So he kept riding hard until he reached the foothills well outside town. Only then, gunless, did he stop to search in his saddlebag for a weapon. But Shelley hadn't had the foresight to bring guns for them. Ed Coolidge cursed him and promised to make him pay for that oversight just as soon as the opportunity presented itself. He was still grumbling when he heard the loud drumming of hoof beats no more than a quarter of a mile away. Ed drew back into the cover of brush and held his hand over his horse's nostrils.

Within a few minutes two riders appeared. He recognized Shelley's flop-brimmed hat and flying bandanna, and then his brother's bulky form. Showing himself, he forced them to veer wide of him and finally came to a gasping halt only yards away.

'Damn you, Shelley, you forgot the guns!'

Rudy Shelley, who was only two-thirds Ed

Coolidge's weight and inches shorter, was immediately riled by the harshness of Ed Coolidge's tone. He had just risked his life getting him out of a cell guarded by a wary old lawman. He had spent six hours in town, keeping out of sight, thirsty for a drink, and all he got for his trouble was abuse.

'What do you think I should have done, Ed – gone into a store and try to buy two more guns, and maybe explain that the prisoners in the jailhouse would want them for later when they busted out?'

Ed Coolidge glared furiously at him, but his brother Leke, who had quickly regained his breath and looked composed enough now to break into song, said easily, 'Ease off, Ed. Rudy did his job good, real good.'

'And he forgot the guns,' snarled Ed.

'So he didn't bring guns. The thing is, we're out and we've got a long way to travel. So either you put a halter on your temper or go to hell on your own, like you did coming out of that stink hole of a town.'

Ed Coolidge straightened, his fury now directed at his older but smaller brother. 'How's that, Leke? What do you mean by that, eh?'

'I mean you didn't give a damn about anybody

else when the town crowd bunched up on us, Ed. You headed out just as fast as you could.'

'I had no gun, damn you!' Ed hotly defended himself.

'Neither did I, Ed. But forget that for now. Rudy says the shack is only a day's ride away and these horses are fresh. We can outrun anybody following. What we've got to do is keep even tempers with each other. Tom's already on his way, and when he reaches us he'll decide what's best to do about things.'

Rudy Shelley drew away from Ed and came alongside Leke. But he still regarded Ed Coolidge warily, knowing the savagery of the man and the hotness of his temper. Rudy Shelley had seen Ed Coolidge kill two men just for bumping him in the street in Laredo. So he had no doubt that he'd kill anybody who got in his way to even the slightest degree.

Leke, seeing from his brother's grumbling that the heart had gone out of Ed, led the way across a barren slope and then called on Rudy Shelley to lead. When they took their positions and Rudy Shelley had his horse galloping strongly, Ed Coolidge, still seething, settled down to follow, keeping an eye on their back trail.

When Gus Ivers cleared the jailhouse boardwalk, he didn't know where to turn. But when he saw a group of townsmen coming down the street, with Billy Owen leading them and running hard, he retreated into the shadows on the opposite side of the building to the laneway. Sweating and choked with a thirst he couldn't do anything about, he dropped back in the shadows at the rear of the town and found a doorway to hide in. He stood there, quivering, more sorry for himself than he had ever been, until he remembered that the horses he had stolen would have been taken to the livery stable yard. Gathering his wits, he made his way to the stables where he saw the Coolidge brothers and another man swing away from the blast of townsmen's guns. Retreating again, hardly able to breathe, and frightened of what might happen to him, he saw Durant clear the jailhouse laneway and head down the back street of town. Alone and defenseless, and knowing he was in no condition to run and keep running, Gus Ivers nevertheless decided he couldn't stay. Sheriff Cavill had fired a wild shot at him, and Ivers had leaped over him, hesitating in the doorway long enough to see Cavill's bloodied head drop to the floorboards.

Ivers waited until the townsmen withdrew under a blast of temper from Deputy Owen before he stole into the night yard and quietly saddled one of the horses. Then, walking it a quarter mile down the back street, he headed out on his own. Strangely, his thoughts turned to Blake Durant, who struck him as a man who knew how to handle tricky matters. If he could find Durant and latch onto him, he might get some benefit from his confinement with two of Tom Moran's cold-hearted killers. With luck and a certain amount of cunning, he might stay with Durant long enough to get himself established properly.

Sweating and looking about him in dread, Ivers went into the dark night.

Blake Durant slowed Sundown a mile from town and waited in the deep darkness, listening to the noises of the night. A dull rumble of activity still echoed out of Sunfish Creek, but he doubted if Billy Owen would give chase that night. Owen would most likely, as the lawman in charge, want to do things so the end result would establish him permanently. So Blake thought he'd collect a posse, arm it, provision it for a long manhunt, and then come on relentlessly.

When Blake smelled the trail dust which told him the Coolidge brothers and their friend were ahead of him, he decided to branch off their trail and head west, parallel to them. In the morning, in the clear light, he could come down from the heights and pick up their trail. That done, he had a big job ahead of him before taking them back to Sunfish Creek. That accomplished, he could see no reason why Billy Owen could continue to make accusations against him. His innocence established, he would be allowed to go on his way, and that was all he wanted.

Moving into the deeper blackness of the foothills, he let Sundown pick his own way. The wound in his side was a dull ache, but the rocking in the saddle didn't bother him too much. In the morning, with a considerable distance put between himself and the town, he would tend to it. Reaching down, he was relieved to find that Owen had not emptied his saddlebags after searching through them. His money was in the top drawer of the jailhouse office where Cavill had put it, but Blake Durant didn't worry unduly about that. He was free now, and he had something definite to do. When it was done, he would make arrangements for more money to be sent from home. Then his drifting could go on, and he could again continue his attempt to forget the past.

Riding along, he began to think about the last two years. It seemed to him that he was constantly destined to meet trouble of some kind face-on. Why? Had he, since leaving his ranch, became trouble-prone? He had known men like that before, men who for no clear fault of their own were always in trouble of some kind. It was as if fate had picked them out. Had he become one of them?

A frown rutted his broad brow. For months now Blake Durant had done a lot of personal soul-searching. He had minded his own business, yet he'd always found somebody needling him, crowding him. So maybe he had changed. The carefree rancher, with his future well decided, was dead. In his place was a man on the drift, a man escaping from his past.

Blake reined in suddenly. His ranch was no more than two hundred miles to the north. Two weeks of easy travelling would see him at the porch, greeted by his brother. Neighbors would soon gather to welcome him back, people who understood what he'd been through. But did they know completely? Could anybody understand that the sight of a petite woman, a blue parasol, a broad-brimmed garden hat, a smile on pert lips, deep-blue laughing eyes . . . any of those could take a man back to times when the world was his, when lifelong happiness had been assured . . . to times when a buckboard had left a dusty trail and a woman had died, leaving a void no friends, no business, no ambitions could fill?

Sundown pawed the ground under him and Blake leaned forward to rub the big black's shoulder. Could he face the return home yet? He didn't know. Even if he could, if he had finally forgotten enough to face the kind but unwanted sympathy of neighbors, this was not the time for it. He had broken out of jail and a lawman had been killed. A deputy would brand him as an accomplice in the crime and hunt him down. He couldn't just ride away and hide and wait for the inevitable day of exposure. He was compelled to stay and work out this business until he could throw off the shackles of suspicion and clear himself.

Then ... perhaps then ... his drifting would be over. The time might have arrived when he could close his eyes at night and the pictures of her wouldn't hurt so brutally. But Blake Durant couldn't be sure as he let Sundown go on.

FOUR

THE POSSE TRAIL

Deputy Billy Owen was unusually calm. Sheriff Lew Cavill's body had been placed on a bunk and covered with a blanket. The doctor had been called to certify him as dead, and funeral arrangements had been made for the next day. Owen had expressed his regret that he wouldn't be on hand to pay his last respects to Lew Cavill because he had pressing business on his hands. He didn't elaborate on what that business was because he didn't have to. Since the slaying of Cavill and the subsequent trouble, nobody had even bothered to ask him what he planned to do. The townsmen involved in the shooting, their number swollen now by many others disturbed by the shooting but too late to get into it, had stood in the jail-house, mutely listening to him, offering no suggestions whatever, in no way attempting to question his authority. Billy Owen knew from this, that he had arrived. This town was his. All he had to do was catch the killers, run down Tom Moran, and from that moment on he'd be a big man.

So he had selected his posse, told them what provisions to pack and where to be at the appointed time. Now, as he stood at Cavill's desk and stared at the blanket-covered form of the dead sheriff, a smile played on his wide mouth. He felt no remorse because of Cavill's death. For months now Billy Owen had known that Cavill had outlived his usefulness. He had become frightened of death. He had slowed down. He wasn't able to make definite decisions. He had slunk back into the background. For a man who had always been so deeply respected, Billy Owen decided that Cavill, in a way, was better off dead. Owen checked his gun and the rifle he had taken from the wall cupboard. Then, putting boxes of cartridges into his pockets, he left the jailhouse.

It was five-thirty in the morning and the posse

was waiting. Looking at them, Owen decided they were a solid enough bunch. Walsh from the saloon had come along, mainly, Billy knew, because Walsh had lost face when knocked out and robbed by Sei Petersen. Jimmy Henmore had come to town late last night, riled by the theft of his two horses. Finding Gus Ivers missing along with one of his horses, he had no hesitation in offering his services. Then there was Bull Marner from the freight yard, a man likely to do some hell-raising himself at any time. If it came to a killing business, Billy Owen knew he could depend on Marner. The others were townsmen who had loved and respected Lew Cavill, and their hate for these killers they would now hunt down, would keep them on their toes. In all, Billy Owen decided, it was as good a bunch as he could have selected himself.

He walked to his horse and swung up, then he gave a brief nod and led the way out of town. Despite the early hour a large crowd had gathered to see them off, and Owen basked in the glory of leadership. He was positive that before a week was out, he would walk the streets of Sunfish Creek as the most important man in it.

*

That night Blake Durant had a recurring nightmare, one which had so often torn his nights apart. In his dream the accident which had killed Louise Yerby so long ago had not happened at all. That, in fact, after he had ridden away, overcome by sadness, she had recovered and was waiting at home for him, watching the horizon, praying for his return. She wouldn't be able to contact him, nor would his brother.

Blake awakened in a cold sweat with the harsh sunlight in his tired eyes. He realized that he had overslept. Pushing his memories away, he saddled Sundown and without wasting time for coffee and food, he rode off. Coming down from the heights, he was especially careful to check the country near Sunfish Creek. Six hours of riding the previous night had put a lot of distance between himself and the town. He hoped it was enough, because he wanted to be the one to find the Coolidge boys and their sidekick and bring them to justice.

Feeling bone-weary, Blake Durant's emotions went dead inside him and he kept his mind fixed on the trouble ahead. He had no doubt that Ed and Leke Coolidge had broken out of jail without time to get their guns, but they would probably be

51

armed now and somewhere ahead, watching the back trail. If they saw him, they would know he was hunting them and they'd lay in wait, biding their time for the chance to cut him down from ambush.

He decided his best chance of survival was to stick to the timbered slope, where his hide coat and tan trousers would fade into the background of brush and tree bark. But he had to make sure that those he hunted were still going west. Coming out of the shadows of the hills, he worked his way down to the prairie. It took him only some fifteen minutes to pick up the tracks of three horses which could not have passed that way earlier than the previous night. Going back into the hills, he rode patiently, always on the alert. For four hours, until the noon heat forced him to take a rest for Sundown's sake, he pressed on, cutting down slopes and climbing Sundown to timbered sections.

He checked behind him now because he knew Billy Owen would be out after the escapees. And Owen wouldn't come alone, despite Blake's suspicion that the deputy would want to tie this matter up personally.

The sun was doing its work when Durant was

rounding a rocky butte. The timber suddenly thinned out and there was dangerous naked country ahead. He reined up and drew his gun. Then, as he came out of cover, a gun barked. The bullet whistled close to his head. Durant wheeled Sundown around and was out of the saddle, letting the black run. Then he caught the glint of sunlight on a gun barrel only fifty feet from him. His gun swung and bucked in his hand, the bullet ricocheting from the top of a boulder. Durant pumped off shots wildly. A man's head went suddenly from sight, then his body appeared, bent over, as he ran towards a horse tethered behind yellow brush. Blake fired, aiming for the left knee. The man let out a howl of pain and pitched forward, onto his face. But no sooner had he hit the ground than he scrambled up and, limping, dragged himself to his horse. Blake waited in the shade of the last of the trees and wondered why the fool had been so impetuous. If he had waited another minute, he would have had a perfect target.

The man pulled the horse about and used it as cover as he scrambled into the saddle. But the effort to climb up was too much for him. Blake fired another shot and the horse reared and tossed him off. The man landed on the side of his head and let out another cry of pain. He lay on the ground on his stomach, his eyes aflame with venom. He lifted his gun from the dust as his horse tore off, then he began to pump off shots. Blake Durant waited as the bullets thudded harmlessly into the tree trunk which he used as cover. When the silence settled again, he moved forward. Sundown came out of the timber but didn't follow him.

When Blake was within twenty paces of the man, the hellion lifted his gun again. Blake couldn't be sure if the man had emptied his gun, so he snap-fired. His bullet hit the man's wrist, snagged off the butt of the gun and entered his neck. He made a brief gurgling noise before his head dropped to the sand. As he died, the loud drumming of hoof beats sounded on the other side of the wide clearing. Looking that way, Blake saw two riders charge into the shallows of the winding river and disappear over the rim of a long slope beyond it.

Blake turned the dead man over with his boot and recognized him as the one who'd opened the cell door to let them out. This man had murdered Lew Cavill, so he felt no remorse at having killed him. His only regret was that he couldn't question him about the attack. Clearly the man hadn't wanted to do it, so he must have been pressed into it by the Coolidge boys. But why?

Blake couldn't find the answer. He whistled for Sundown and the big black came trotting up and stood quietly while he mounted. Blake made for the slope, crossed the creek and went up the other side, knowing he was making an easy target of himself. But when he reached the rise, he saw the two riders disappearing into the sun-soaked distance. Blake reined up. Maybe Ed and Leke Coolidge were unarmed, he thought. The man who'd freed them from jail might have had the only gun in the group, which was why he'd been watching the back trail.

Blake flicked sweat from his brow with a finger. If Billy Owen was close by, the sound of the shots would have carried to him and would make him press on harder. So Blake kneed Sundown along. Open country stretched before him, but he knew he had no chance of catching up to the Coolidge boys before sunset.

When daylight was gone, he made camp on a rock-studded slope and slept.

*

'Damn him, damn him to hell!' growled Ed Coolidge. 'Why in blazes did Tom sign him on?'

Leke Coolidge nodded, his thoughts on Rudy Shelley identical with his brother's. Rudy Shelley had just about committed suicide back there, panicking and firing his first shot before Durant was an easy target.

'Why'd he have to mess it up like that, Leke? Hell, now we got no gun at all – and Durant's coming after us for sure. It's us he wants.'

'Whinin' ain't gonna help, Ed. We'll just have to make do with what we got.' Leke's voice was calm, although his brow was deeply rutted and his mouth was pinched tight. The strain of the ride was beginning to tell on him, but unlike Ed he had the ability to accept things and make the most of them. It had been like this all his life, following Ed into one piece of trouble after another, and then getting him out of it. In the beginning he'd tried to change Ed, but it was impossible. Ed was born the way he was.

Now Ed made a disgusted sound. 'What we got, damn you, Leke, is two worn-out horses and some water. What we ain't got is grub and guns. And we've also got Durant breathin' down our necks.'

Leke snorted. 'To hell with Durant! He's only

one man, and anyway he can't catch us before we reach the cabin. Rudy said there were guns there in the cabin plus just about everything else we'll need. Then Tom will arrive and we'll be just fine.'

Ed glared sourly at his brother's optimism. He was about to say something sarcastic, but the look on Leke's face was enough to tell him that words would be a waste of time. Scowling, he went back to his horse, swung up and growled, 'Well, let's get to that blasted shack as soon as we can. I don't feel right without a gun in my hand.'

Leke, although uncertain if his horse could take much more of this hilly country, climbed into the saddle and followed his brother along the hill trail. It was dusk. Soon it would be full dark and Durant would have to stop or lose their trail. If almost anybody but Durant was following, they probably would have made camp. But Durant was tough – and he had a gun.

Jimmy Henmore, Walsh from the saloon, and Bull Marner, who had left his freighting business to become involved in the excitement of the manhunt, unsaddled their horses at the creek while the rest of the posse looked for a good place to spread their bedrolls. Only Billy Owen remained in the saddle, reluctant, despite the hard day behind him, to give up his search for even a few hours. He studied the men carefully, then he decided their tempers were frayed and they would need sleep before going on.

With a sigh, Owen finally succumbed to the weariness in his bones. Four or five hours of sleep wouldn't be a waste if it meant each member of the posse would awaken in a better frame of mind and show as much willingness to hunt down the sheriff's killers as they had when leaving Sunfish Creek. After unsaddling his horse and ground hitching it for the night in lush grass near the creek, Billy Owen removed his gunbelt, shirt and hat, and hung them over a low branch of a cottonwood. He then knelt at the side of the slow-running stream and washed himself from head to waist. Feeling the weariness falling off him, he put his shirt on over his wet skin and fitted his hat to his head. He stood then, thinking about the Coolidge boys and Blake Durant. So far they had come across the tracks of three horses, so he discounted the possibility that the old rascal, Gus Ivers, had come along with the others. He knew too that he had gained ground on the three in front. But one small worry niggled at his mind.

It had been Walsh who'd found the dead man a few miles back. It was clear from the sign that the man had hidden in ambush, and that his bushwhacking attempt had failed. Billy Owen allowed that the place of ambush was as good as he would have picked for himself. How then did the fool fail? And who had killed him? One horse had approached the dead man, and one man's boots had left marks in the dust near the body.

Walsh had suggested that ahead of them were only two men, the Coolidge brothers. Who, Walsh had asked, was the man who'd shot the third fugitive? Marner had then asked some questions about Durant, wanting to know what manner of hellion he was. Billy Owen, unable to supply definite evidence against Durant, had cut Marner short, telling him he'd find out soon enough.

Sitting alone now, watching a couple of townsmen get a fire started, Deputy Billy Owen thought about Durant. His doubts about the man still had considerable substance Durant had come to Sunfish Creek across the desert, riding a trail from Willoughby, where Tom Moran belonged and would surely return after his release from jail. Durant was no ordinary drifter – even Lew Cavill had agreed on that point. He rode a beautiful black stallion, one of the finest pieces of horse-flesh Owen had ever seen. And Durant carried himself with the confidence of a man accustomed to handling emergencies. His gaze was steady and he was well-built and work-trimmed. That part worried Owen more than a little. He doubted if the usual run of hellion Tom Moran associated with, would do honest work of any kind. Also, when confronted with the charge of complicity with Tom Moran, Durant had calmly stated his case and asked to be taken on trust. In short, Durant had acted like the kind of man he'd claimed to be.

Owen scrubbed a hand over his trail-grimy neck and cursed himself for not having washed more thoroughly. He liked to be scrubbing-brush clean, his skin tingling. To hell with it, he thought. He could clean up properly when he returned to town with the posse. Soon he would be killing men, adding more notches to his gun, gaining more respect from the townsmen.

'Coffee's ready, Deputy,' came a call from the fire.

Owen gave a nod but didn't move. Durant still worried him. There had been no time to check out Durant's story. He had come in well-dressed, clean-shaved, riding his big black horse, confident and well-heeled. Yet, when breaking out of the jailhouse, Durant had knocked him down. Owen's right hand moved across his jaw, which was still slightly swollen. His lips were cut inside but weren't swollen. Perhaps they had bruised a bit and this might show. He cursed under his breath, for he was vain and didn't like showing the scars of defeat. Well, Durant had won the first round. Durant had knocked him unconscious and had then ridden off unscathed.

Getting to his feet, Billy Owen averted his face from the glare of the fire. He took his coffee and a plate of beans. Then, moving deep into the shadows, he sat and ate moodily, unable to get Durant out of his mind. Finally he decided that, come what may, Durant would be made to pay for attacking him and escaping from custody. Owen, lost in his thoughts concerning the drifter, had completely forgotten that Lew Cavill was dead.

His meal finished, Owen left his plate and coffee mug beside the fire for somebody else to clean, and announced, 'You men get four hours' sleep. No need for anybody to stand guard because there's no likelihood that we'll be attacked. After you've rested and the horses are fresh again, we'll push on and use what's left of the night to close in on these killers.'

With that, he moved across to his gear, stretched out on the ground and closed his eyes. But he couldn't sleep. Excitement ran through his body. This manhunt could establish him as a first-class lawman. Avenging his sheriff's death, in the eyes of the town, would make him a man of great substance, a man equal to meeting all the problems associated with keeping Sunfish Creek free of crime and violence.

FIVE

LISA MORAN

'Well now, Leke, look-see what we've got here.'

Ed Coolidge's sun-scorched face creased in a grin as he drew rein and looked down the barrel of a rifle held by a slender, dark-haired young woman. It was two hours after sunup, and their ride through the hills to the hideout had almost been pleasant. The fact that he was within reach of a gun and provisions had caused Ed Coolidge to relax to the point where, only moments ago, he'd been whistling a gay tune. Now he pointed a finger at the young woman as his eyes greedily devoured her slender, well-shaped young body.

Leke said, 'We're friends of Tom Moran, ma'am. We just came outa the Sunfish Creek jail. Man name of Rudy Shelley helped us.'

The young woman lifted her head a fraction and leaned back on her heels. Seeing that they carried no guns, she felt confident she could handle them.

'Where is Mr. Shelley?' she asked, her voice matching the calmness of her gaze.

Ed Coolidge leaned back in the saddle, still grinning. 'Rudy, do you mean, ma'am, the feller who got us outa jail? Rudy didn't make it.'

A slight trace of worry showed in the young woman's eyes. 'What do you mean, he didn't make it? He hasn't been hurt, has he?'

'About as hurt as a man can get, ma'am,' Ed told her. 'He's dead.'

The young woman, obviously shocked, lowered the rifle until it was in a line with Ed Coolidge's chest.

'We rode into a slice of trouble, ma'am,' Leke went on. 'But we reckon we're a few hours ahead of it now, and we're real hungry. What's your part in this thing?'

She eyed them both sharply, her lips slightly pinched.

How much could she trust them? she asked herself. The younger of them seemed all right, with his quiet talk, but the other one, the bigger man frightened her. She didn't like the look in his eyes as his hot gaze roamed over her body.

'I'm Lisa Moran,' she said finally. 'Tom Moran is my father. Mr. Shelley met me in Lightning Springs and told me that my father had finally been pardoned and was coming out of jail within a few weeks. I insisted that he bring me here so I could wait for my father. When Dad comes, I'm going to make a home for him wherever he wants to go. I intend to help him forget the injustices done to him and make up to him as much as I can for the discomfort those people caused him to suffer.'

Ed Coolidge's eyebrows arched and he regarded her with new interest. 'Tom never mentioned havin' no kin, ma'am,' he said. 'Never heard a word from him about havin' a girl like you.'

'Well, I'm his daughter – nothing can change that. And who are you?'

'We're the Coolidge brothers, Miss Moran,' Leke put in, aware that Ed was studying the girl in a way that annoyed her. 'This is Ed, my brother.

I'm Leke. We rode with your father lots of times, and we're here to do what we can for him.'

'He won't want to see you,' she said. 'I told Mr. Shelley the same thing when he said he was riding into Sunfish Creek to meet you. My father isn't the terrible man he's said to be. Perhaps he's made a few small mistakes, but then he was probably influenced by the likes of you. I want you to leave this place right away and never come back. When my father gets here, I'll tell him I've rented a store in a small town a long way from here, and he can become a gunsmith again.'

'Gunsmith?' Ed asked her incredulously. He glanced at his brother to see what effect the girl's words had on him and saw that Leke was as surprised by the idea of Tom Moran being a gunsmith as he was himself.

She said, 'Yes, Mr. Coolidge, a gunsmith, and one of the best. My father learned the trade during the war years. That's the only interest he'll have in guns from now on, I promise you.'

Ed scrubbed a hand across his face, hiding his grin. 'Ma'am, I'll admit that Tom is real fancy with a gun, but ain't you kinda takin' things for granted, making all those plans for Tom without talkin' to him about it first?'

'No, I'm not taking things for granted, Mr. Coolidge. I'm merely taking things into my own hands. My father left me with friends down south, but he wrote often. He told me of his ambitions and his plans. Those letters were not written by a man who's said to be an outlaw – they were written by a man who'd been led astray by others. But now that he's paid the penalty for his foolishness and rashness, I'm sure he'll come along with me. So, you see, there is no use at all in your staying.'

Ed whistled through his teeth, but Leke, after a warning glance in his direction and a slight shake of his head, muttered, 'Ma'am, be that as it may, we'd kinda like to hear it from Tom himself. On top of that, we've travelled hard and far and we're dead beat. We've also got no grub and no guns.'

'There is food and guns,' Lisa said. 'Take what you want.'

Leke nodded to this, but Ed still seemed inclined to argue. They slid out of their saddles, then Lisa backed quickly away as Ed moved towards her. Grinning, Ed stepped past her and entered the small cabin.

On the table were four handguns and a box of shells. There was nothing else of interest in the room. Going to the guns, Ed selected one and tested it for balance. Satisfied with its weight and feel, he loaded the cylinder. He then filled his pocket with shells and stepped aside to let Leke arm himself. Seeing Lisa standing at the door, he said:

'What kind of grub you got?'

Lisa shook her head. 'I'm not sure. I've only had coffee since I've been here. I'm not able to eat, I'm so impatient to see my father again.'

'Well, I'm kinda impatient to see old Tom, too,' Ed said easily. 'But not so damned much that I ain't gonna get rid of this hunger that's gnawin' at my guts.' He crossed the room and rummaged among the boxes on the two shelves. He found enough provisions to last a few men a month. Hacking open a can of beans with a knife, he emptied the can onto a plate and forked the beans greedily into his mouth. Leke opened another can, sat on a box and ate.

Lisa watched them with distaste as they wolfed the food down.

'You a good hand at makin' coffee, girlie?' Ed asked through a mouthful of beans.

'I'm not 'girlie', Mr. Coolidge. My name is Lisa Moran. Please, while you're here, which I hope will not be long, use that name.'

'Sure, sure, Lisa,' Ed said. 'But get some coffee boiling, will you? I've got a thirst that's burnin' me up.' He looked around. 'No likker, eh?'

'Certainly not! Mr. Shelley wanted to bring some, but I refused to allow it. My father won't want any, I'm sure of that.'

Ed grunted at this, but went on eating. When he finished his second can of beans, he pushed his plate away and rummaged among the provisions again. He found a jar of peaches, and, using two fingers, rammed the fruit into his wide, bean-stained mouth. Lisa again studied him with disgust, but she said nothing as she set the coffee pot down on the old stove. Soon these two would be gone. She felt sorry about Rudy Shelley being killed, but she didn't want to know the details of his death. From the moment she'd heard about her father's release, she'd been determined that violence would never be part of his life again.

When the coffee was ready, she poured herself a cup and left the pot to simmer on the stove, so the two men could help themselves. Then she went outside, mainly because the air in the small room was rapidly becoming filled with the stench of the brothers. Looking out across the barren country, she wondered why her father, a free man again, would select a place like this to come to. Why hadn't he gone to a town and sent for her? His last letter, written in prison, had told her that he'd been framed, and he'd hinted that soon he'd be coming home to her. Lisa, too excited to wait, had packed and boarded a stagecoach to Willoughby, where she'd sought out the man mentioned in the letter, Rudy Shelley. Her father had written that Shelley would send her some money as soon as possible.

Rudy Shelley had turned out to be a grimy, unimpressive man, with shifty eyes and a habit of kicking the ground with the toe of his boot when he talked to you. But he had quiet manners and he'd done everything she'd asked until he'd ignored her plea to forget about contacting her father's former friends.

Well, she told herself, Shelley had paid for his folly and now she was in the company of the Coolidge brothers. But only for the moment. Just as soon as they'd eaten and taken what provisions they wanted, she would insist that they move on. She was certain they would comply with her wishes, for she suspected that they feared and respected her father.

'It'd be best not to be standin' in the doorway, Miss Moran,' Leke Coolidge said now as he moved out to inspect the rocky terrain which surrounded the cabin. Ed followed his brother out, wiping his mouth on his grimy sleeve. The reek of him made Lisa's stomach muscles tighten. She moved quickly away, spilling some coffee down her white blouse.

Ed, pulling the bandanna from his neck, stepped to her side. 'Here, Lisa, let me help you.'

'Keep away from me!' Lisa cried, bumping against the cabin door in her anxiety to get away from him.

She spilled more coffee and this brought a raucous laugh from Ed Coolidge, who caught at her wrist and pulled her roughly to him. He quickly rubbed the bandanna pad down the right side of her bosom. Lisa gave a cry of alarm, broke free and slid along the wall and threw the coffee mug at him.

Leke turned, eyes filled with annoyance. 'Damn you, Ed, can't you leave her be?'

'Nope, Leke, I can't leave her be, not her with her uppity ways. I kinda got a yen to hold her some, and maybe more. Pretty, ain't she?'

'She's Tom's daughter!' Leke said angrily.

'Touch her and he'll kill you.'

'Mebbe,' Ed said casually. But he made no further attempt to follow Lisa. Leaning against the wall of the shack and grinning broadly, he watched her intently.

Lisa, her cheeks flushed, hurried away, but she had only reached the corner of the cabin when Leke Coolidge called out:

'Miss Moran, don't go any farther. I don't want you walking about. That white blouse of yours can be seen a good distance away.'

Lisa peered at him. 'Why worry about that?' she asked. 'If my father saw me from a distance, it would make him hurry all the more.'

'Ain't him I'm worryin' about, ma'am,' Leke said tightly.

'Who then?'

'Other folk.'

Ed had made himself a cigarette and was now puffing at it, his eyes still fixed greedily on her.

Lisa waited until Leke walked up to her before she asked, 'What other folk, Mr. Coolidge?'

'Folks who're huntin' us, ma'am.'

Lisa gaped at him. Heat rose in her face and she felt a prickling of fear at the nape of the neck. 'Hunting you? Who's hunting you and why?'

Leke worked his hands under the buckle of his gunbelt. Standing there, he looked like a little boy caught at mischief. 'Well, it's got something to do with Rudy Shelley and Sunfish Creek, Miss Moran. You see, after Rudy got us out of jail, the law in that damn town started to shoot at us. Rudy was forced to gun down the sheriff, and by now there'll be a big posse out after our hides. So, you see, you've got to keep out of sight. We left no good tracks for 'em to follow here, so if we play our hand smart we won't be worried by 'em. Then, when your pa comes, we'll work something out.'

Lisa glared at him. 'My father will want nothing to do with killers like you! Go away now, please!'

Leke shook his head. 'Can't do that, ma'am. We've got to wait for Tom. We've been waitin' a long time for him to get out. Now that he's free, I guess we'll be the ones he'll want to see most.'

Lisa, shocked, backed away from Leke. The inference in his words hadn't escaped her.

Ed now stood nearby. Suddenly she was frightened. She walked along the wall. As Ed lunged at her, she avoided his groping hand and ran. Ed started after her, but Leke caught him by the shoulder in an iron-fisted grip. When Ed glared at him, Leke said:

'It's Tom we came to meet, Ed, not a woman.'

'You go to hell, damn you! I want to take some of the sauce out of her.'

'For that, Ed, Tom'd kill you.'

'You mean he might try. But maybe Tom ain't what he was before they put him away. How come he was loco enough to hire a coward like Shelley? And how come his daughter's here messin' up things? How are we gonna take Sunfish Creek apart with a damn woman along?'

'Tom doesn't even know she's here, Ed,' Leke said. 'When he finds out, he'll know how to handle it properly, you'll see.'

'What about Shelley then? How come Tom pulled him into the outfit?'

'Shelley made only one mistake, Ed,' Leke reminded him. 'He got us out of jail and he killed Cavill, didn't he?'

'He was a damn fool and he got what he asked for,' Ed snapped, his desire for Lisa temporarily forgotten. But then he heeled about as he heard a cry from the brush beyond the small clearing.

They looked at each other and Leke said, 'We've got to get her back, but don't maul her any. As soon as we settle with Sunfish Creek, you can have all the women you want. But not her, Ed, not Tom's girl.'

Ed's eyes were smoldering with anger as Leke ran past him and headed for the end of the clearing. Lisa's cry suggested to him that she had stumbled and perhaps hurt herself. He hoped she wasn't badly injured because if Durant or the posse caught up with them, he didn't want to leave her behind. At the same time he didn't want a burden on his hands if they had to run.

Breaking into the brush, Leke saw Lisa's white blouse in a thick patch of vines and yellow brush. He ran to her and was about to reach down for her arm when Lisa turned quickly, fear in her wide-set dark eyes. There was a tearing sound as the blouse was caught on a thorn. It ripped away from her, exposing her milky breasts. Leke couldn't help but stare, a quick intake of breath coming from him. Then he felt a hand on his arm and Ed was beside him, his face twisted with desire.

Leke flung his arms out to keep Ed back. But a growl came from Ed and he shoved his brother off-balance. Ed was reaching for Lisa when Leke drew his gun and snapped:

'That's it, Ed. That's just about far enough.'

Ed jerked around and saw the gun leveled at

him. 'How's that?' he snarled. 'You callin' me to draw, brother?'

'I'm telling you to back off, Ed. You're only gonna make more trouble for us than we can handle. Anyway, she's hurt. Leave her be.'

Lisa struggled to her feet and covered her lush breasts with her hands. She leaned to one side, favoring her right ankle and looking down, Leke could see that the ankle was already swollen.

Taking advantage of Ed's silence, Leke asked, 'You hurt your ankle, Miss Moran?'

'Yes.' The word was no more than a breath from Lisa, who couldn't tear her terrified gaze from Ed's wild-eyed face. His heavy breathing sent shivers down her spine and she wanted to kill him. She had never felt such thorough hate and loathing.

Leke said, 'We'll carry you back. Maybe it ain't all that bad. But you've got to give us your word – no more running off. We ain't gonna hurt you, either of us. I give you my word on that.'

'Your word?' Lisa snapped back angrily. 'Am I supposed to accept that?'

'You've got no choice, ma'am,' Leke said. He reached out, adding quietly, 'Now just rest on me. Ed'll go on ahead.'

Ed held his brother's stare for a long moment, aware that Leke's grip on his gun was firm and the hard glint in his eyes was not pretence. Leke would shoot him for sure. Deciding he could wait, Ed walked back through the brush – and into the blast of a gun.

SIX

HARD TRAIL TO FOLLOW

Blake Durant knew he was being followed from the moment he broke camp on the second morning out of Sunfish Creek. He didn't see or hear anything, but an instinct born of experience made him positive of pursuit. Then there was Sundown's nervous throwing of his head at times.

Blake watered the black at a small creek, feeling he was being watched. Then he galloped Sundown off. The horse, refreshed by a night's rest and eager to run, was a handful to slow atop the rise, but Blake managed to drive the big black into thick brush. He was out of the saddle within half a minute of clearing the slope. He stood with his hand over Sundown's nostrils.

Blake didn't have long to wait before Gus Ivers, long gray hair flying from under his flop-brimmed hat, rode over the rise at full speed. Ivers was some fifty yards down the next incline when he realized he'd lost his quarry. He drew rein and sat his horse, looking anxiously about him. His eyes were red-rimmed and his clothes were caked with sweat.

Blake swung back onto Sundown and came out of the brush. He knew he had nothing to fear from Gus Ivers.

When Ivers saw Blake, his lined face brightened with relief. 'Hell and damn you, Durant, but you took some catchin'! I been trailin' you for some twenty-four hours now. I saw that feller's body back there and figured you'd settled with him. But what about them other two?'

'They're still ahead.'

Ivers sent his troubled gaze over the heat-hazed land ahead. 'Yeah? How far ahead are they, do you reckon?'

Blake shrugged. 'Maybe a few hours. Not far.'

Ivers licked his lips and worked his neck about inside the grubby collar of his threadbare shirt. Then he raked his hair with one hand while he beat the dust from his hat with the other against his knee.

'You – you're set on catchin' up with 'em, Durant?'

'Yep.'

'Why?'

'They'll help clear my name. I don't aim to ride on with a charge of killing a lawman and breaking out of jail hanging onto my tail.'

Ivers was silent for a while. Then, eagerness in his voice, he said, 'But hell, you don't need them to prove your innocence, Durant. You got *me*. We can double back and meet up with Owen and I'll tell him how it all happened.'

Blake gave a wry smile. 'Ivers, Billy Owen hasn't much time for you. No matter what you said, he wouldn't believe you. You forget you're a convicted horse thief who just broke out of jail.'

Ivers glared angrily at Blake. 'Hey now, Durant, no need for you to get on that bandwagon. I mistook a couple horses for my own. That's it in full, and I ain't havin' nobody, not even you, callin' me a damn—'

'Forget it, Ivers,' Blake said, impatient to move on. His stare roamed ahead, past the open stretch of barren country. Somewhere in that wasteland were the two men he sought, and he didn't see how Ivers could be of any help when he caught up with them. He added: 'Stay here and wait for Owen to come up. I'll leave a clear trail.'

'To hell with that!' snapped Ivers, mopping heavy sweat from his drawn face with an ancient bandanna. 'Maybe you're right about Owen not taking to me. And hell, what with Cavill dead, who knows what kind of meanness he's burnin' up with? No, Durant, you just got yourself a trail partner.'

Blake studied Ivers gravely for a long moment. Getting away from a shrewd old trail campaigner like Ivers would take a lot of doing. He pulled Sundown about, studied the country behind them again, and then he said, 'Okay, but I'll be setting a fast pace, mister. If you can't keep up, too bad. And for hell's sake watch what you do when we sight the Coolidge boys. They aren't about to sit down and parley with anybody, least of all us.'

Ivers' skin went gray under his tan, but he gave no answer. Blake, still worried about him and uncertain how he would act in a gun battle, concentrated on the trail ahead. He remembered how Ivers had cleared out of the jailhouse as soon as the Coolidge boys had been freed. At that time Ivers had been worrying only about himself.

Letting Sundown have his head, Blake led the way across the barren stretch. Half an hour later, halting in the shade of a huge boulder he inspected the ground. The horse tracks he'd been following had petered out. Leaving Ivers to watch the trail behind, he scouted in a circle without success. Coming back to Ivers, he said, 'I don't think they went past here.'

Ivers frowned. 'Why in hell not, Durant? What in thunderation would they stop here for? There ain't nothin' here but rocks, lava pits and rubble. There's hardly any shade and nests of rattlers.'

'You know this area?' Blake asked.

'Been through it once or twice, but I sure ain't stopped to admire the scenery. It's twenty more miles to Toby Ridge and no water or shade between.' Blake came out of the saddle and Ivers added: 'What the hell are you gonna do now, Durant? Hell, them two brothers are desperate, ain't they? And they must know they're being followed. They ain't gonna just sit about and wait to be caught.'

Blake hardly heard him. His stare swept the country above them, trying to pick out even one upturned stone that might indicate the direction in which the Coolidge boys had gone. But only the sun-scorched emptiness of the rocky heights met his searching gaze.

'The way I see it, Ivers,' Blake said at length, 'the feller who helped them break out of jail was one of Tom Moran's friends. Since they came this way and not towards Willoughby . . . well, maybe they're not going to meet Moran in a town where everyone can see what's going on.'

'They're gonna meet Moran out here, do you mean?' Ivers asked.

'I think so, old-timer.'

Ivers gulped uneasily and wiped his brow with his soiled bandanna. He shifted in the saddle and looked uneasily about, as if expecting a horde of attackers to suddenly materialize and descend on him. 'Then . . . then we'd best push on, eh, Durant? Hell, maybe it's a good idea to just forget about them. If we wait about, Owen'll catch up with us and all hell will break loose. We can cross the border and get settled someplace else, you and me, working as a team. I ain't outlived my usefulness yet, Durant, not by a long shot.'

Blake shook his head. 'I want the Coolidge boys. Until I find them, Owen will be annoyed as hell because I belted him a couple of times, and of course he'll connect me with Moran and the Coolidges. No, I'm going up to check in those hills. You can ride on if you like.'

With that, Blake Durant sent Sundown up the rocky slope, riding slowly and carefully between boulders and around dry brush, all the time searching the ground for a trail. An hour later he stopped on a ridgeline to rest and watched Ivers struggling up the last of the long slope towards him.

When Ivers reached him, the old man slid from the saddle and collapsed on the ground, exhausted. 'Durant, I been collared by some ornery fool critters in my time, but you sure take the first damn prize. If you keep up this pace, we ain't gonna have the strength to draw a gun against them jaspers, let alone fire the damn thing.'

Blake didn't reply. The climb had been hard on man and horse, and a study of Ivers' face told him that the old man was close to the point of giving in.

'You'd better rest up,' Blake said. 'I'll go on and see what's up farther. I should be back in about an hour. If I don't get here, you'll know I ran into something.'

Gus Ivers lifted his head from the boulder face he was settled against and sighed wearily. 'There's just no stoppin' you, eh, Durant?'

Blake shook his head. Gus Ivers muttered something under his breath, then climbed painfully to his feet and refitted his battered range hat over his long, shaggy hair. Then he said, 'Well, if that's the case, I guess there's no use doin' it harder than we've got to. This is the halfway point to the shack.'

Blake spun away from Sundown and regarded him acutely. 'Shack?' he repeated.

Gus Ivers nodded guiltily and pointed to an area beyond a ragged line of cliff face. 'Back of that. I reckoned you'd come this far and give up. But you ain't the kind who gives up easy. More fool me for trailing along with you.'

'Is this the only way to reach the shack?' Blake asked.

Ivers shook his head. 'Nope. The best way, or the best as I remember it five years back, was the way Tog O'Brien blazed up them heights from the other side. The trick is to ride past the hills and instead of heading in to Toby Ridge, to circle way back and tackle it from the other side. But it's a tricky business, what with that side gettin' lashed by freak winds, and when the rains come, there are washouts and ruts that'd hide a mule team. Old Tog didn't take much to other folks' company, kinda just wanted to hide away by himself. My horse broke its leg out here once, and Tog took me to his shack and let me stay till we saw a wagon train crossing the Toby Ridge trail. Then he took me down to the trail junction and left me there and I didn't see him again, didn't much want to either. Tog O'Brien was maybe not the kind who'd see a man left in bad trouble, but he made no bones about not wantin' friends droppin' in on him.'

Blake felt annoyance rising inside him, but he controlled it when he realized that using the other trail to the shack might give him an advantage if the Coolidge boys were holing up in the shack.

'You want to stay or come on?' Blake asked the old-timer.

In answer Ivers dragged himself back to his horse and took up the reins. After a pained look at the steep, rugged country ahead, he raked his neck with a grubby hand and muttered, 'I ain't stayin' here alone, that's for sure. Old Tog's ghost is bound to be snoopin' about protectin' his bones.'

Blake pushed on. For the next two hours, with several spells to rest the horses and let Gus Ivers regain his strength, he led the way up, step by painful step, until finally he stood on a narrow ledge, bare wind-swept rock below him. It took several minutes for Blake's eyes to grow accustomed to the harsh sun glare, then he saw the roof of the shack protruding from a sheer wall of rock. He moved along the ledge for a better look at the shack. It was a small structure with a dusty-paned window on the near side. The land around the shack was as barren as a plate.

Blake drew his gun and checked it. Behind him, Gus Ivers came up the last few yards of the incline and then gave a long sigh as he sat on the ground. Blake turned. Ivers was peering over the rim of the rocky ledge. His face was haggard, but his eyes were alive with fear and the expectation of trouble.

'See anybody, Durant?'

'Not yet.'

'Well, maybe they ain't there. Could be that you didn't find their tracks into Toby Ridge because you didn't look good enough. Maybe they did go on.'

Blake shook his head. 'They're here; I feel it.' He holstered his gun and looked about for some windless shade for their horses. Soon he found a space between two huge boulders. Pushing the horses into position, he spoke to Sundown and the big black dropped his head and stood there quietly. Returning to Ivers, he found the old man kneeling, still looking down. Ivers had drawn his gun. He glanced anxiously across at Durant, gulped uneasily and muttered:

'I heard something, Durant.'

'What?'

'Hard to say. A scratch of noise. Could have been a voice.'

Blake hunched down and studied the barren country below. The wind flattened clumps of brush, adding its eerie sound to the feeling of desolation. But there was no sound that didn't belong here.

Long minutes passed and Blake began to grow restless. It wasn't like him to wait for things to happen.

'I'll take a look,' he said finally, drawing his gun. But he had taken only one step when Ivers gave a sharp cry. Blake froze. The brush some thirty feet below suddenly parted and Ed Coolidge came pounding through, his mood clearly ugly.

Blake went into a crouch, shading the barrel of his gun from the sun glare with his left hand. Ed Coolidge was two steps clear of the brush and glaring back across his shoulder when Gus Ivers pumped off a shot. Blake swore as Ed Coolidge dived for the ground, and pulled his gun clear of leather.

'Damn you, Ivers!' Blake snapped, then Ed Coolidge sent three bullets up at him. One of the slugs tugged at his sleeve as Blake went forward.

Then Leke Coolidge came charging out of the brush, dragging a young woman with him. Her blouse was torn, revealing her breasts, and there were scratch marks on her neck and arms. Leke Coolidge shoved her forward and dropped beside his brother. The young woman fell to the ground and struggled to her feet. She looked anxiously at the Coolidge boys before she glanced fearfully at the slope above and broke into a limping run. Ed Coolidge let out a shout and fired a shot after her, but the woman paid no heed. She reached the shack and disappeared from sight around the corner.

Blake Durant had in the meantime made his way several feet down the slope and crouched, Ivers just behind him. The Coolidge boys fanned their guns, but the shots were wild. Ivers slithered down beside Blake and said hoarsely:

'Hell, Durant, we got 'em! Only thing they can do is head back into that brush. We don't have to move an inch from here.'

As Ivers finished speaking, Leke Coolidge jumped to his feet and began to sprint across the clearing. Ivers let out another sharp cry and punched off shots. Leke Coolidge went down on one knee and then pawed at the air as though trying to keep his balance. With a triumphant cry, Ivers put another bullet into Leke. The hellion's forehead was ripped open. He fell back and his legs gave a dying kick.

Ed Coolidge was running now. He hurdled his brother's body and went on. Blake triggered four shots at the ground in front of Ed and called for him to stop. When he didn't, Blake directed his fifth shot at his leg. The bullet struck home and sent Ed Coolidge sprawling. He hit the ground, rolled to his feet and limped out of sight.

Blake heard Ed hammering on the door of the shack as he scrambled down the slope. He lost his balance at the bottom and fell. Slugs tore at the ground near him and he was forced to back off and take cover behind a rocky ledge. There was no sign of Ivers. Blake waited. The hammering continued and then stopped. Hearing a sound behind him, Blake turned to see Gus Ivers sliding down the slope on the seat of his pants. When it seemed he had to crash into Blake, his boot heels dug in and the momentum of his slide brought him to an upright position. Off-balance, he wind-milled his arms frantically in an attempt to stop himself from falling into the clearing and had just about succeeded when Ed Coolidge put a bullet through Ivers' neck.

Gus Ivers' old body collapsed without a sound. When Blake knelt beside him, the old man gave a last fluttering gesture with his hand and lay still.

Leke Coolidge was dead. Gus Ivers was dead. A young woman was trapped yards away in an old shack.

Blake left Gus Ivers and made his way along the fringe of the clearing. There was no sign of Ed Coolidge.

Then bullets slammed into the door of the shack and a moment later Ed Coolidge rode past Blake, his gun bucking. Blake was again forced to dive for cover. When he returned his gaze to Coolidge, he saw only his back before he disappeared down the slope.

SEVEN

A WOMAN ALONE

Blake knelt in dry brush not far from the shack. It was close to noon and the heat was intolerable. Flies swarmed about Blake's face. 'Ma'am?' he called. There was no answer. 'I'm not one of the Coolidge boys,' he said. 'Leke is dead and the other is on the run.'

'Who are you?' came the young woman's voice from inside the shack.

'The name's Blake Durant. Open the door and I'll explain everything.'

Blake rose and took a step forward. But a rifle blast from the shack window forced him to heel about. From the brush he called, 'Now listen, ma'am, quit that! I mean you no harm. I've trailed the Coolidge boys to here and I don't intend to quit chasing until I've got Ed.'

She cried, 'If you come a step closer to me, I'll shoot you down. I want no part of you or them.'

'Wanting no part of *them*, ma'am, I can understand,' Blake said as he crept closer. He could see the flimsy door now. One good shove would break it down. He said, 'You seemed to have been in a lot of trouble with them, and I can understand your concern for your safety now. But listen to me – I'm on your side.'

There was no answer this time. Blake braced himself, drew in a deep breath, then charged at the door. It took him four long strides to reach it. He put all his weight behind his right shoulder and drove himself at the timber. The door buckled and came off one of its hinges.

Durant found himself a yard inside the doorway. The young woman had backed off to the far wall and was lifting the rifle to her shoulder. Blake lunged at her and knocked the rifle from her grip. The rifle discharged and the slug burned past his arm.

'I said to cut it out,' he roared at her, but she

came at him, her hands raised, her fingers curled like talons. Blake grabbed her hands and held them at her side, but she continued to struggle until he lifted her and carried her across the room. He dumped her on a bunk against the side wall and stood back, a scratch mark on his right cheek.

Lisa Moran glared up at him, plenty of fight still in her. She seemed unaware that her full breasts were partly exposed. Blake picked up a towel from the end of the bunk and flung it at her, then he crossed the room, picked up the rifle and pumped the remaining shells from it. He hurled the rifle against the wall and walked to the doorway.

'We'll talk after you've changed that blouse,' he said.

He heard the bunk springs squeak and then light footsteps on the bare boards. He turned. She had her back to him as she pulled another blouse over her head. He turned away, wondering how far Ed Coolidge would run. Blake frowned. If he took this young woman along, would she slow him down too much? No matter. He couldn't leave her out here in the wilderness.

She looked at him. 'You say your name is Durant?'

'Blake Durant, ma'am.'

'If you have anything that resembles decency in you, Mr. Durant, you'll leave now. I want no part of you or anybody else.'

Blake touched the scratch on his cheek and then studied her closely. 'I'll leave in good time, ma'am. But first, who are you and what were you doing here with the Coolidge boys?'

She thrust out her chin. 'I do not feel obliged to answer any of your questions, Mr. Durant, nor do I care what you are after or why. I ask only that you leave me alone.'

'That won't do,' Blake said. 'This is wild country, and it's no place for a woman on her own. Were you here when the Coolidge boys arrived?'

'I was here, yes, and for reasons of my own. Now I want to stay here – alone.'

'What if I leave and Ed Coolidge doubles back? Do you figure you can handle him?'

'I'll barricade the door,' she said firmly.

Blake smiled wryly. 'From what I know of Ed Coolidge, little things like a barricade won't stop him getting what he wants. Did you have an earlier connection with him that I should know about?'

Lisa glared furiously at him. 'I had no connection whatever with him or his brother or anybody like them, thank you. And I don't want any connection with you. I merely want to wait here until my – '

Lisa stopped suddenly and a flush rose in her cheeks. Then she sucked in her breath and looked angry at herself. She glanced at the rifle on the floor but made no move towards it.

'Two men are dead, ma'am,' Blake said sharply. 'I'll have to bury them. While I'm at that chore, you might think things over because, whether you like it or not, I'm not going to leave you out here alone for Ed Coolidge to find again. I should think you've had enough of him to come along quietly.'

Not waiting for her answer, Blake stepped into the harsh sunlight. He was only halfway to the body of Gus Ivers when Ed Coolidge suddenly rode out of the brush, his gun barking. Blake spun about, his Colt coming quickly into his hand. Ed Coolidge rode on, his face flushed, his bullets whining close to Blake – too close for him to stand his ground. Blake fired back and reached cover in the brush. Then Lisa Moran appeared in the doorway. She put a cartridge into the rifle and pressed the stock to her shoulder. The Winchester bucked. Coolidge turned his horse and charge at her. He jumped out of the saddle to land within a foot of her. He grabbed her and, using his horse as a shield, roughly hurled her across the saddle. When Lisa struggled, he rapped his gun butt against her head and she went limp. Back in the saddle, he emptied his gun at Blake Durant and then drove his horse back to the brush at the far end of the clearing. Blake held his fire, frightened that he might hit the girl. Helpless, he watched Ed Coolidge ride off. Then he was scrambling up the slope and heading for Sundown. When he freed the big black, he led it to the top of the rise and stared down into the vast expanse of wild country between him and the prairie. There was no sign of Ed Coolidge or the girl. He waited for Coolidge to negotiate the slope and come out on the prairie. He had to be sure in which direction Coolidge was going, but although he waited for a full five minutes, the hellion didn't appear.

Troubled, Blake led Sundown and Gus Ivers' horse back to the shack. There he hitched them to the rack and spent some thirty minutes burying Gus Ivers and Leke Coolidge. That done, he turned Ivers' horse loose, unsaddled, and then he started after Ed Coolidge. He knew this wasn't going to be a simple matter of finding Coolidge, besting him with his gun or fists, and returning with him to Sunfish Creek. Ed Coolidge had the girl. This meant Blake Durant would have to ride a quiet trail and place his shots carefully – if he got a chance to shoot. And all the time Deputy Billy Owen was getting closer.

Following the clear trail left by Ed Coolidge. Blake rode into the afternoon heat.

Billy Owen was surly as he stopped in the shade of the two rocks on the rocky slope that led to the mountaintop. With his posse packed about him, he watched Walsh, the saloonkeeper, inspect the ground between the two huge boulders. Walsh turned and informed him that two horses had been there.

'The only other thing I can work out,' Walsh told the deputy, 'is that they were here maybe an hour or so ago.' He walked from the shade and checked near the ledge of rock. Grinning, he pointed out other marks in the ground, saying, 'Seems two men waited here, one of 'em lying flat. Then the sign shows that they went down the other side.'

'We'll follow them, Walsh,' Billy Owen said as he put his horse into a brisk walk.

His surliness persisted when he saw the steep slope on the other side, a section that he couldn't possibly ride down. Sliding from his trail-weary horse he walked forward until it became necessary to crouch and sidle through a narrow gap between a ring of rocks. His horse dragged on the reins, clearly afraid of the descent, but Billy Owen had his eyes fixed on the slide marks of boots in front of him and he pulled the horse along. A moment later the horse pulled free and in sudden panic leaped across a deadfall log and went down on its side. Owen ran to the animal and grasped the reins. The horse kicked out and whinnied in fear until Owen, sweating and cursing, worked the animal to its feet.

'If a horse gets that way, it's best to blindfold him,' Walsh said from close behind Owen, but all he got for his suggestion was a grunt.

Owen went on, his horse stumbling. By the time he reached the bottom, he was exhausted. Hitting the horse hard on the rump, he let it run and stood there with his drawn gun, glaring about him.

The posse came to him in a straggly line. The

men were trail-dusty, raw-eyed and clearly worn out. Jimmy Henmore was the first to walk past Owen. When the lawman snapped at him wanting to know where he was going, Henmore, a huge cowhand with a sharp temper, merely glanced at him and walked on. Owen strode after him but pulled up short when Henmore drew an unsaddled horse from a clump of brush and turned it around, inspecting it.

'One of mine,' he said, and Owen, scowling, left it at that. Henmore brought the horse to the front of the shack and told Walsh, 'Seems like old Gus got at least this far. Must've near killed him.'

Hearing this, Billy Owen growled, 'You sound sorry for that damn old horse thief, Henmore. How come?'

Henmore, giving a twisted smile and shrugging, answered quietly, 'I've always been sorry for old Gus. He's the kind that can't help himself at times. When a man's got as little as Gus Ivers has, I guess he's just got to take what he sees to improve his lot. I bear no grudge against him, Deputy.'

Owen's brow knotted deeply and the youth went out of his face. He looked suddenly wearier than any of them, as if worn out by something hacking away inside him. 'Well, I've got a thing or two against him, Henmore. Ivers broke out of jail and was one of four men who killed Sheriff Cavill. Maybe you figure that's not enough reason for you to hunt him down and bring him back to trial?'

Henmore shrugged again and settled against the hitch rail. 'Owen, you're pushing yourself too hard. The way I see it, you're getting your wires crossed. Gus Ivers couldn't kill a steer let alone a man. He'd pass out at the sight of blood.'

'Well, he didn't pass out when he saw Cavill killed, damn you, Henmore,' Owen growled. 'He ran and he ran fast, and he got away with your horses.'

'Only with this one,' Henmore corrected. 'The other's back in town, so I reckon I got what I came for. As soon as I rest up, I'm heading back.'

Owen glared at him, and his shoulders squared. 'You're backing out, Henmore?'

'Yep, Deputy, that's exactly what I'm about to do. I guess in the beginning I was willing to go all the way, but two days of you is plenty for me. You're making this more than just a manhunt, mister.'

'I'm making it what? Say it straight!'

'Sure.' Jimmy Henmore had been building a cigarette while he was talking. Now he put the cylinder in his mouth, thumbed a match alight and lit the cigarette. Swallowing smoke, he looked straight at Owen.

'I don't know, Deputy, but I've got a feeling you don't really care too much about Sheriff Cavill getting killed. I reckon you're a lot more interested in running down Tom Moran and his crowd. And, from what I've been told by some of the other men here, you're barking up the wrong tree with Durant. He isn't involved in this the way you make out.'

Owen, livid with rage, held his gun tightly, and his breathing quickened. 'Durant broke out of jail, Henmore. Before he got away, he belted me down. Then Durant rode off with the Coolidge boys, and I'm saying it loud and clear that Durant came to our town to be on hand when Tom Moran rode in to get even with Lew Cavill and myself.'

'I hear Durant claimed he never even heard of Tom Moran, Deputy,' Jimmy Henmore put in.

'He claimed that all right, but Sheriff Cavill and I didn't believe a word of it. But that's no concern of yours any more, Henmore. You've pulled out, so go on your way.'

Jimmy Henmore straightened and squashed his cigarette between his stubby fingers. For a moment, Walsh and Bull Marner thought Henmore was going to take the business further. Then, giving Owen a faint smile, Henmore turned away. One of the posse members who'd been inspecting the shack suddenly appeared in the doorway, holding a saddle in one hand and a torn blouse in the other.

Holding the saddle up for Henmore's inspection, the man said, 'It's got your brand on it, Jimmy.'

As Henmore reached for the saddle, Owen brushed past him and snatched the blouse from the townsman.

'What the hell is this?'

'Found it inside, Deputy,' the man answered. 'There's some other lady's clothes too, and a comb, a hair brush and them kind of things. Also, there's a store of guns and grub enough to keep half a dozen people fed for weeks.'

Owen frowned heavily for a time, then he shouldered past the man and stormed into the shack. He found two other posse men searching about and ordered them outside. Then he made his own search of the cabin, looking confused.

Walsh pointed out the smashed door and the bullet-riddled walls. 'What with all that and the torn blouse, seems some woman's got herself into trouble. Which pair do you figure we've been trailing, Deputy?'

'Who the hell can say?' Owen answered curtly. 'We've got nothing to go on, have we?'

There was a shout from down the clearing where another of the posse members was standing just short of the edge of the brush. His face reflected concern as he signaled. Owen and the others made their way down. The man, a store man, lean and drawn, pointed into the brush.

'Two graves,' he said.

Owen pushed forward, knelt and felt at the earth mounds. 'Fresh,' he said. 'Get a shovel, somebody.'

'What . . . what do you aim to do?' asked Walsh.

'Dig 'em up, what else? We've got to know who they are – the Coolidge boys, Durant, Ivers or maybe a woman. If it's a woman, I reckon we're on the trail of some real bad ones.'

Walsh drew back, shaking his head. 'Not me, Owen. I'm not diggin' up no graves, not on your life.'

Owen glared at him as he straightened up. 'Damn you, Walsh, are you out to mess up this whole business? I said somebody fetch me a shovel. I'll do the digging if you lily-livered towners can't.'

Two men went off and returned moments later with a rusted spade. Dirt on the blade indicated that it had been used to dig the graves. Owen quickly scooped up dirt and soon he exposed the gray face of Gus Ivers. Jimmy Henmore worked his way to the grave and breathed a curse. Then he knelt, smoothed the gray hair back from the old-timer's face and said something that nobody heard. He then came upright, glared at Billy Owen and walked towards the horse Gus Ivers had stolen.

To the horse he said, 'I wish you'd carried him a lot farther than this.' Then he stepped up and into the saddle and rode to the horse that had brought him here. In his eyes was the mist of memory, and in his mind were thoughts of good times gone by . . . good times that were fast being buried under the heels of men like Billy Owen. He decided that he didn't like Billy Owen. So he rode off, leading his horse.

At the site of the two graves, Billy Owen uncovered the face of Leke Coolidge. He brought back his boot as if to kick the corpse, but his foot went down as Walsh said:

'Easy, Deputy. He's a dead man.'

Owen glared over his shoulder at Walsh, then he looked away, lowering his head. He punched his fist against his palm and muttered under his breath, his face dark and strained. His lips were a thin line.

'That makes three dead,' said Walsh.

Bull Marner gave Walsh a nudge. While Billy Owen glared down at the dead face of Leke Coolidge, Marner drew Walsh away from the circle of men.

'He crazy?' Marner asked in a tight whisper.

Walsh shrugged, 'Seems like he's settin' about this business like Henmore said.'

'I don't like it,' Marner said.

'You ain't alone in that, Bull. One of the Coolidge boys is dead, meanin' the other one ain't gonna be easy to take. As for old Gus . . . hell, he wasn't so bad. Why should somebody want to kill him?'

'If old Gus travelled this country with anybody,' Marner said, 'it wouldn't be with the Coolidge boys. And by the look of the horse he rode, he did it hard. What about him and Durant together?

You reckon it could have been that way?'

Walsh turned slowly. He saw the horse tracks, the downtrodden brush, the bullet-riddled wall of the shack and the ruined door. Then he said, almost as though to himself, 'We followed two riders up the mountain on the other side, and we found this place was the scene of a gun battle, with two dead and a woman in trouble. And as far as we know, there ain't anybody in front of us but Ed Coolidge and the Durant gent. But I don't reckon they're together, like the deputy wants us to believe. What do you say, Bull?'

Marner shook his head. 'Hell, I don't know. But what about Tom Moran? He's had time to reach this place, ain't he? Been out two days now, they say.'

Walsh scratched the hair at the back of his neck. Suddenly he wanted to be in his saloon, exchanging small talk with his customers and taking their money. Being out in this wilderness, with Billy Owen driving them like a madman, didn't suit him at all.

Making a sudden decision, he muttered, 'Come on,' and made his way back to Billy Owen, who still stood alone near the graves.

'Deputy,' Walsh called as he drew up.

Billy Owen jerked his head around, his stare fierce. He didn't answer, but his gaze went to Bull Marner and then back to Walsh.

'Deputy, we've got a slant on this business that I think you should listen to.'

Owen's shoulders tightened under his range shirt, but he didn't reply.

Having taken the bit between his teeth, Walsh continued, 'I figure Durant ain't no part of the Moran crowd, Deputy. If he was, who in blazes is making all the trouble out here? There isn't anybody but Ed Coolidge on the loose now, along with Durant. And Ed wouldn't have killed his brother, would he? Although he wouldn't think twice about killing off old Gus Ivers. So it stands out as plain as the sun that's burnin' the hides off us that Durant, after locking horns with you, saw that his only chance to clear himself of murder and jail-break was to follow the Coolidge boys. If he could bring them in, then he could convince you and the rest of us of his innocence. Gus Ivers likely rode with him, and those were their tracks that came over that ridge line. They found the Coolidge boys here with a woman, then there was one hell of a fight. Ivers got his and so did Leke Coolidge, then Ed rode out with Durant on his tail.'

'You're loco,' Owen snapped at him. 'There are no clear signs that anything like that happened.'

'Then why is there so much killing if Durant's one of them? Do you reckon maybe a skinny old man like Gus Ivers came out this way to take them all on?'

Bull Marner watched the reaction of the other men to this and was encouraged to back up Walsh by what he saw in their faces. Walsh had made an impression on them to a man.

Marner said, 'I don't see how it could be any other way, Deputy. So what we've got to do now is try to catch up with Durant and talk to him. No sense in going in with guns cocked and making trouble we could easily avoid.'

Owen glared at the big freight operator. He had never had much time for Marner, but he'd kept his distance and had treated him with kid gloves because of Marner's position of influence in the town.

'Has Durant got you scared, mister?' Owen barked.

Marner scowled back. 'He sure ain't Deputy. I'm scared of no living man, so don't get fool ideas about that. I don't even know Durant. I only saw him the once, when he drew rein on that big black of his outside your jailhouse. But damn it, now that I recollect, he didn't strike me as any trouble-maker on the push. To me he seemed to be just an ordinary stranger riding in, a feller on the drift. He looked over our town like it didn't mean a damn to him.'

Owen smirked. 'Which just goes to show how blind you are, Marner, and maybe stupid, too. Just leave the detection of outlaws and hellions to those trained to spot 'em, will you?'

Bull Marner's body seemed to grow taller and powerful muscles bulged on his bare forearms. Walsh moved to his side and muttered:

'No need for all this. We've got things to do besides standing here and squabbling. Sheriff Lew Cavill is dead and we ain't no closer to knowing who killed him. Till we get that settled, I reckon we all should work together, listen to each other, exchange ideas.'

Owen snorted at him. 'Do you figure we should sit down and have a conference, Walsh? Should I let you men tell me what to do and how to do it? Maybe you want my badge, too, eh, here and now?'

'Nobody's said it's come to that, Deputy,' Walsh

put in quickly. 'I'm only saying that – '

'You've said too damn much, mister. I'm running this outfit and if anybody else is like Henmore and doesn't want to follow my orders . . . well, he can ride back to town. I'll go on alone if necessary – but I'll get all of Lew Cavill's killers and I'll bring what's left in for trial.' Owen turned and looked at the rest of the posse. 'For now, you men get some rest. Our horses need a spell of a couple of hours at least. We'll eat, too, and then we'll get after 'em.'

With that Billy Owen heeled about and took long strides to the shack. Entering the building, he drew in a ragged breath and looked fiercely about the small room. He could feel the respect of his men fading. His authority was being questioned. How had it happened so suddenly? He couldn't see where he'd gone wrong. By pushing the men hard, he'd proved himself to be an able leader. He'd brought them to within an hour or two of the men they hunted. If a couple of fugitives got themselves killed, what did it matter to the men?

Cursing under his breath, Owen dropped down to the bunk. He could smell the scent of a woman in the room and for a time he wondered what she looked like. Then he dismissed all thoughts of her from his mind and closed his eyes. He was dog-tired, just as his men were.

EIGHT

TOM MORAN

When she opened her eyes, the sky was like a pink pearl, with no clouds in sight. For a moment Lisa Moran thought it was morning. She didn't know where she was until she tried to move her hands and found she was tied to a deadfall log. Then realization hit her with frightening clarity. Her face burned with shame and outrage. Ed Coolidge had taken her down the mountain and then over rough country that jolted her with every stride of the horse. She remembered him dragging her from the saddle and letting her fall to the ground. She'd lain there, scratched and bleeding where rocks and brush had torn her flesh. She was bruised on the back, neck and ankles, and her stomach felt as though somebody had been punching at her for hours. She had tasted the salty earth and had heard him moving about, fear like a stone in her stomach.

'Now,' he had said as his hands gripped her shoulder and turned her over. Then he tore her clothes and she had clawed at his face until he'd backed off. He'd stood there, glaring at her insanely while she adjusted her dress and waited for his next assault. When he'd attacked her again with renewed viciousness, she had screamed. He had struck her again and again until unconsciousness claimed her.

Lisa Moran realized that it was not morning after all, but sundown. She pulled on the ropes which held her wrists but Ed Coolidge had bound her securely and she could do no more than burn her wrists. So she stopped struggling and looked around. She was in a small clearing with a huge boulder behind her. The deadfall log was to her right, and near her feet was the charred remains of a fire. Ed Coolidge wasn't to be seen. Lisa lay there and tears streamed from her eyes and stained her cheeks. Then she began to sob.

'Shut up, damn you!'

He was back. There he was, standing near the end of the log, stretching his neck and shading his eyes to check on something beyond the clearing. The sound of brush breaking cut into the late afternoon's stillness and Lisa turned her head in the hope that she might hear more. Ed Coolidge took his gun from his holster and thumbed back the hammer. The viciousness in his face sent a chill through Lisa and she knew that he meant to kill.

Licking her cracked lips, she swallowed hard and then screamed. Ed Coolidge wheeled about, his face filled with hate. His gun was trained on her.

'Damn you! I shouldn't a wasted my time on you.'

The brush behind him suddenly parted and Lisa saw a huge black stallion charging through. Riding the animal was Blake Durant. Ed Coolidge fired at her and missed, then he had no more time for anything but to meet Durant's challenge. He dropped down into a crouch and pumped off five shots. The bullets caused Sundown to veer off and the black's head, bobbing up and down momentarily, kept Durant from firing. He drew

Sundown to a skidding halt and wheeled him about. By then Ed Coolidge had run for cover. Blake jumped out of the saddle, cast one look at Lisa and then he went after Coolidge. He followed the sounds of the outlaw's flight through the wild country until suddenly he was in another clearing, Below him, the country was wild. Huge boulders and thick clumps of trees met his searching gaze. But now there was only silence as daylight faded.

To go on meant to risk running into an ambush. With night coming, Coolidge would be able to get away. Troubled, Blake Durant stood there, listening, hoping for one sound that would help him capture Coolidge. To take him alive was still his plan. He needed the hellion. Even if Ed refused to talk, the act of bringing him back might be proof enough of his innocence.

But the sound didn't come. Blake retraced his steps to the first clearing. Lisa tried to struggle free of the ropes again and now blood ran down her wrists. She looked up at Durant as he knelt at her side and with two quick knife slashes cut away her bonds. He then took her hands, turned them over, and went to his saddlebags. Taking out a jar of healing salve, he returned to Lisa and helped

117

her to her feet. He rubbed salve on the rope burns while Lisa stood rigidly, amazed at the tenderness in his hands. She couldn't take her eyes from his face as he worked, and when he released her hands, she stood there, tears running down her cheeks.

Blake studied her torn clothing and understood what had happened. He said, 'Rest here. It'll be dark soon. I'll try to find a pool where you can wash up. Barring that, I have enough water.'

With that, leaving her staring after him, Blake Durant went into the brush. He had no great hopes of finding a pool in this section, but knowing the misery that can come into a person's life he realized that this young woman would welcome some time to herself to compose herself and collect her thoughts. So he walked silently through the gloom of dusk, ears still cocked for a sound from Ed Coolidge.

Lisa Moran quickly composed herself. She tidied herself as best she could and treated the scratches with the salve Durant had left with her. That done, she raked at her hair with her hands, lamenting the fact that she hadn't brought a comb along with her. She knew she must look a terrible mess.

She sat down and thought of the terrible things that had happened to her. All she had wanted was to come out here, meet her father and take him home. Instead, she'd been among killers and brutes, animals of the worst kind. She had been abused and beaten and subjected to unspeakable atrocities. Tears began to form in her eyes again and she lowered her head and let them run down her cheeks. She knew that she was now unfit to be a wife to a decent man. Ed Coolidge's mauling hands seemed to be on her. She shuddered and burst into sobs.

A sound from behind her caused Lisa to straighten. She looked back and saw Sundown, but beyond him a man was riding slowly towards her. Her first terrifying thought was that Coolidge, dodging Blake Durant, had doubled back. She rose, her legs shaking.

The man came on, then his horse emerged from the deep shadow. Lisa gaped and almost collapsed with shock.

'Pa? Is it you, Pa?'

'Lisa!'

She broke into a run, tripped over the deadfall log but quickly scrambled to her feet. Running on, she grabbed at her father and clung desperately to him. Tom Moran, in clothes that hung on his thin body, placed a skinny hand on her head and rested it there as a deeply troubled look came into his sunken eyes.

'Now, now, girl, quit that. Won't help either of us.' He peered beyond her to the small clearing and seemed puzzled. When Lisa stepped away from him, wiping her eyes with the sleeve of her tattered, soiled blouse, he said, 'I heard some shots not long back.'

'Oh, Pa . . . Pa!' Lisa suddenly broke down and Tom Moran, for all his weariness, slipped out of the saddle and pulled her to him. He patted the back of her head.

'Easy now, girl. By the look of you, you've had trouble enough. But I'm here now. Pull yourself together and tell me about it. Was it a man?'

'A swine, Pa, a filthy animal. He . . . he . . .' Again Lisa broke down.

Tom Moran pressed her closer to himself. Fury began to build inside him. His two years in prison had been hard. No man had served his time harder, for word had been sent ahead to the prison authorities by Cavill and Billy Owen. They'd branded him as a murderer despite the ruling of the court at his hearing. There had been daily beatings, periods of starvation and solitary confinement. Finally he had given up trying to fight them. He had lived only for the moment of his release, the moment of his revenge. Now his girl was here, where she shouldn't be, the victim of a rapist.

'I want to know everything, girl,' he said finally. 'I'll have it fixed. First tell me how you got here and why you came. I left word with Rudy Shelley to see that you had money and that you stayed home till I got there.'

Lisa drew back from him and dabbed at her eyes. She looked intently at her father and was suddenly ashamed of her concern for herself. What had happened to her could be forgotten in time, in a great deal of time. But meantime, her father looked terrible. He was an old man. spent before his time, little more than a shadow of his former robust, proud, forceful self.

'Just the bare facts, girl,' Tom Moran said as he led his horse into the middle of the clearing. He inspected the huge black stallion that belonged to Blake Durant. But the long years of prison had taught him patience. He kept his gaze away from his daughter so she could concentrate on her story, and Lisa, still shocked by his pitiful condition and his ragged, ill-fitting clothes, settled down on the deadfall log and spoke quietly.

'Mr. Shelley is dead, Pa, or so I was told.'

'How come, Lisa?' Moran's voice carried no emotion whatever.

Lisa told him how she had gone with Shelley to the shack before Shelley had left to meet Ed and Leke Coolidge in Sunfish Creek. Tom Moran accepted this as if he already knew that part of it. She went on, 'Then those Coolidge men came and said Mr. Shelley was dead. I told them to take provisions and guns and leave me alone. But Ed Coolidge made it plain that he . . . he wanted me. When he attacked me, I beat him off and ran, but he and his brother caught me in thick brush when I stumbled and hurt my ankle. They dragged me back to the shack. Then Mr. Durant and another man, an old man, arrived.'

'Durant?' Tom Moran said.

Lisa frowned down at her swollen hands. She still didn't have a definite opinion about Blake Durant. She said, 'He's a big man who said he was in jail with the Coolidge brothers when Mr. Shelley rode in and got them out. He said the sheriff had been killed during the break and he was chasing Ed and Leke Coolidge to take them back and clear his name.'

Tom Moran looked sharply at her. 'Go on,' he prompted when he saw a different light in his daughter's eyes. It had been a long time since any woman had shown herself to him in that way, but he could remember the softness in Lisa's mother's face on the rare occasions when he did something that pleased her. He wanted to know more about Blake Durant.

'Well, Pa, when Mr. Durant arrived, there was a lot of shooting. I broke away and ran for the shack so I didn't see very much of it. But later, after Ed Coolidge had ridden off, I learned that the old man who'd come with Mr. Durant was dead, and so was Leke Coolidge. Ed Coolidge returned, knocked me out, threw me onto his horse and brought me here.'

Lisa was on the point of crying again when her father straightened and stared at her with what Lisa thought was disbelief in his eyes. 'Ed did that?'

'Yes, Pa.'

Tom Moran pointed at her torn dress. 'He did that, too?'

Lisa bit her lip and lowered her eyes. She

couldn't answer him.

'Did Ed Coolidge *take* you, girl?' Tom asked suddenly.

Lisa looked up, frightened by the bitterness in his voice. She saw his face was livid and his lips colorless. More hate than she had seen in any man's face was there before her, and she was suddenly frightened of what her father would do.

'It's over, Pa. He's gone.'

Tom Moran lifted her to her feet and swore under his breath. Holding her hands together at the buckle of his gunbelt, he said quietly, 'Ed was a friend of mine. He rode with me. I'd trust him with anything.'

'We can forget it, Pa,' Lisa said, but Tom Moran shook his head.

'That's his horse?'

Lisa looked at Sundown. 'No, Pa, that belongs to Mr. Durant.' Then, realizing there was more her father should know, she went on hurriedly, 'Ed Coolidge tied me so I wouldn't run off. He meant to hold me as hostage in case Mr. Durant or somebody else caught up with him. Then Mr. Durant arrived again and after some more shooting, Ed Coolidge ran into the brush.'

'Durant crawls out of the ground often, eh?'

Lisa frowned at him, not fully understanding the bitterness in his voice. 'He . . . he's hunting Ed Coolidge, Pa. I believe what he told me. He wants to clear his name. He's saved me twice now and as soon as he gets back.'

Lisa stopped as a sound came from the other side of the small clearing. Her father flung her aside and drew his gun. His face was filled with hate again, and he looked a stranger to her, a man frighteningly vicious. He had always been gentle with her and with the people she knew, which was why she could never believe the stories about him. Yet, looking at him now. . . .

Blake Durant stepped out of the gloom on the other side of the clearing and stopped dead in his tracks. Lisa heard the click as the hammer of her father's gun went back.

She called out, 'No, Pa, it's Mr. Durant! He's done me no harm. He means you no harm either.'

Tom Moran stood with his feet planted wide apart and his scrawny frame rigid. His eyes were narrowed so that his face was tightly puckered.

'Keep comin', Durant,' Tom Moran called out, and Durant walked slowly across the small clearing, watching him intently. He was seeing Tom

Moran for the first time. Despite the man's slight build and ragged clothing, he detected an air of confidence in him that warned him to be wary.

Durant stopped just short of Lisa, keeping Sundown within reach.

'My daughter's been telling me about you, Durant,' Moran said. 'Seems I'm obliged to you for the couple of times you've helped her. But don't get the idea that will change things between you and me.'

'What *is* between us, Moran?' Blake asked.

'I ain't sure, mister. So you start explaining yourself to me. What's with you and the Coolidge boys?'

Blake told him matter-of-factly about his imprisonment, the wrangling with the Coolidge pair in the cell, the breakout, and his subsequent hunt for the brothers.

Moran listened intently, not interrupting, and Lisa kept studying Blake Durant in a way that left no doubt that her gratitude to him was boundless.

'So you hate Owen's guts, too?' Moran finally asked.

Blake shook his head. 'Maybe he was just doing his duty as he saw it. He's obsessed with running you down and tying down all your trail friends. But as for hating him – no, I don't think that's the feeling I have, Moran. He annoyed me and I want to bring him down to size and make him see things as they are.'

'And what about me, Durant?' Moran growled, shifting the gun a little higher.

Blake held his hard gaze. 'There's nothing between us, Moran. For mine, you can take your daughter and get to hell out of this area. My business is with Ed Coolidge. I want to take him back alive. Then your daughter can lay whatever charges against him that she feels obliged to.'

Moran grinned thinly. 'Coolidge assaulted my girl, Durant. For that he's gonna die . . . slow, real slow.'

Blake said, 'I need him alive to clear my name, Moran. He's no use to me dead.'

'Too bad, mister.'

Lisa watched each man in turn, hoping that the two of them would not become angry with each other. She couldn't understand why this mattered so much to her.

Blake Durant moved lazily towards Sundown. He caught the saddle and wheeled the big horse around, but when next he looked at Moran, he found the outlaw still had his gun trained on him.

Moran said, 'Not so fast, Durant. I ain't finished with you.'

Blake eyed him coolly. 'I've said my piece. I've got no business with you and you've got none with me.'

'I want to know what Owen's up to, mister,' Moran said.

'He'll be out on the trail some place, Moran, likely getting close. But if you've served your time and they let you out to become a free man again, I don't see what worry Owen can cause you. It's Ed Coolidge he's after, and maybe me.'

'He's after me, damn you, Durant. He's always been after me. He made sure I had a living hell in that damned jail, and he'll go on trying to make hell for me until I shoot his stinkin' guts out!'

Lisa backed away, deeply shocked, but the men ignored her.

Blake said, 'Kill him, Moran, and you'll be right back where you started, won't you? They said there was some doubt about your guilt last time, but there'll be no doubt this time. My advice is that you ride off with your daughter and try to make life a little easier for her.'

'Your advice?' bellowed Moran, shifting the

gun about in a threatening manner. 'Don't start preachin' to me, boy. I've been makin' my own decisions all my life and no cub is gonna start doing it for me. So shut down, do you hear? Shut down!'

'Sure,' Blake said, then he swung onto Sundown. He picked up the reins and turned the big horse around. Moran stepped back, clearly undecided for the moment how to handle him. Then Blake said, looking past him at Lisa, 'You'll be all right from here, Miss Moran. I wish you well.'

With that Blake heeled at Sundown's sides and the big black stepped off. Moran wheeled, his fist white under the pressure of his grip on the gun. But he made no move to stop Blake Durant leaving. It was only when Durant had gone from sight, along the trail Ed Coolidge had taken through the brush, that Moran finally swore heatedly. He holstered his gun and then, signaling for his daughter to go ahead in Durant's direction, muttered:

'No need to hurry. Them two ain't goin' far in that country this time of night. But be quiet, girl. Ed'll go berserk when he learns I'm huntin' him.'

Lisa was unable to move. She stood there, her

face white with shock. All her confidence fell away and she was once again frightened.

She said, helplessly, 'Pa, why don't we go home? Let's get away from here.'

Tom Moran shook his head grimly. 'I've got to find Ed and settle with him, girl. Ed double-crossed me. Then there's Owen. I got to get him, too. You'll understand in time.'

'I'll never understand if you kill anybody, Pa,' Lisa said. 'I could never forgive you for that.'

Tom Moran gave her a tight smile. 'Lisa, it's happened before and likely it'll happen again. You've got to remember that and learn to live with it. Your pa's no saint, that's for sure.'

Lisa felt her knees buckling. 'Oh, Pa,' she called out miserably. 'Then you're . . .' Her voice trailed off and tears ran down her drawn face. She had never felt more broken in her life.

'I'm what I am, no better and no worse, girl. Now quit snivellin' or I'll pack you off on your own. I've got no time to worry about anything else but the men I'm hunting. Come now and you'll see that it'll all turn out OK in the end.'

Moran walked across to his horse and picked up the reins. He watched his daughter impatiently for a time, but when she finally moved towards the brush into which Durant had disappeared, he smiled.

NINE

NO TRAIL FOR COWARDS

Deputy Billy Owen awakened with a start when he heard a noise inside the shack. He jerked himself into a sitting position, his hand on his gun butt. He was bathed in sweat and felt worse than he had before he'd dozed off. Standing in the doorway was Bull Marner, his huge frame blocking the sunlight.

'Everybody else is saddled and waitin', Deputy,' he said.

Billy Owen frowned at him, confused for a

moment, wondering what Marner was talking about. He dropped his feet to the floor, and with his thoughts suddenly clearing, he looked up sharply, asking:

'Some have pulled out?'

'Three. Cassidy, Coombs and Marlow. Marlow's ailing and the others are gonna ride back with him. They didn't figure he'd make it on his own.'

'Damned cowards!' roared Owen and lunged across the room.

Marner stood his ground and shook his head. 'They've got as much guts as the rest of us. But Cassidy shouldn't have come in the first place, bein' too old for this kind of thing. Coombs . . . well, I guess he's doin' what he's always done, stayin' in Cassidy's shadow. And Marlow, well, like I said, he ain't lasted as good as he hoped to.'

Owen studied the big man sourly as he brushed past him, and stopped just outside the shack. Walsh and the other seven men stood in the clearing. Owen realized it was only an hour or so from sundown. He had overslept.

Bull Marner strode past him, swung into the saddle and moved his horse beside Walsh's mount. The two exchanged a look before Walsh led Owen's horse to him. He dropped the reins into Owen's hands and then wheeled away. Within a minute, Owen was leading them away from the clearing, following the clear tracks of horses through the brush. The heat was excessive and it became worse the deeper they went into the tangle of rocks, trees and vines. At times he had to stop and slash brush out of his way, and twice he lost the trail and had to double back to pick it up again.

When the last of the daylight made it impossible to go on much longer, Owen drew rein. Walsh and Marner were soon beside him, Walsh saying:

'We'll never find anybody here. Look down there.'

Owen looked and swore. As far as he could see, the country dropped away. He knew that one false step by man or horse and they'd go toppling down to their deaths. Sweat hung on his upper lip and was lined heavily across his brow.

'*They* made it, didn't they?' Owen said.

'Sure, but in good light. We'll kill ourselves if we try to follow. I suggest that we make camp and tackle it in the morning.'

'And give them another eight or nine hours' start on us?' Owen grumbled.

Walsh puckered his fat lips and shrugged.

'They won't be able to move far either, not in this light. But if you want to go on, go ahead. Me, I'm staying.'

'Be a moon out soon,' Bull Marner put in, looking towards the far horizon where an eerie ring of light foretold the coming of the moon.

To Walsh, Owen snapped, 'You against ridin' in moonlight, saloon man?'

Walsh, who had not noticed the light on the horizon, shook his head. 'Guess not.'

'Then tell the men to stand down, but nobody's to go to sleep. We won't be here for more than half an hour at the most. Then we're gonna ride through the night. By morning I want to be right down at the bottom of that mountain, even if we're the first to reach it.'

With that, Billy Owen hitched his horse to high brush and made his way to a small rock. He sat on it, hands on his knees, and stared broodingly into the distance.

Ed Coolidge dodged a cluster of sharp rocks and worked himself into a sitting position against a tree stump. He slowly drew his left leg up and tore away the blood-smeared legging. The long walk through the wild country had left his shirt in tatters and had broken the heel from his right boot. That misfortune had aggravated the pain in his left leg, until now, an hour after fleeing from Durant's bullets, he could go no farther.

His face went white when he inspected the wound under the faint light of the moon. Durant's bullet had slashed across the flesh just above the knee and taken a huge chunk of thigh with it. Coolidge realized that he must have bled profusely all the time he was struggling to get away.

Thirsty, he sucked at his teeth and looked gloomily about him. He felt trapped. He didn't know how far he'd come or how much farther he still had to go. Even without a horse, he knew he wouldn't be much inconvenienced until he reached the flat country. There he would have to hide out and hope to get a shot at Durant. With the big black, he could get to Toby Ridge easily and see a sawbones. Then he'd keep going and to hell with Billy Owen, Durant and Tom Moran.

Thinking of them brought his thoughts back to the previous night. Moran's hellcat daughter had hardly been worth the effort of the fight. She had left her marks on him, but he'd also left his mark on her. Even if she'd been unconscious all the time, he knew she would never forget what he'd done.

Tearing a strip off his tattered shirt, Ed bound his thigh tightly above the wound and then he put a pad on the wound and bound it in place. Knowing he could do no more to help himself, and desperate for a drink, he pushed himself to his feet and rested against the shoulder of rock. His head was reeling and he felt weak in the legs. But he forced himself to think of what Tom Moran would do to him when he heard of the attack on his daughter, and he summoned enough strength to limp on.

For another hour, getting weaker by the step, he struggled through the wild country. He didn't mind the sharp pricks of pain as brush raked him because it kept him going.

But at the end of an hour, he found himself standing rock-still, on the edge of a precipice, looking down and seeing nothing but blackness. Ed Coolidge backed off, feeling for support. When he touched a tree trunk, he grabbed at it and then sank to the ground. A groan came from him as his weight went down on his left thigh, but then he fell to the side and lay still.

Sweat stung his eyes and was sour in his mouth.

He groped about for a pebble, found one, put it in his mouth and sucked it. Minutes later, the pebble fell from his gaping mouth as his head dropped. Ed Coolidge slept.

Tom Moran talked as he threaded his way down the rocky mountainside. 'You've got to understand how it was in the beginning, Lisa, with your mother ailing like she was. Life was hell. I worked hard on our place, near eighteen hours a day, morning till way past sundown. At night I'd lie beside your mother and listen to her moaning, wondering what else I could do to change things. I'd plant things and the sun'd burn 'em into a crisp. We were always short of water, so we'd wash on weekends only. What few steers we had, plus a couple of milkers, strayed or were rustled. I went to the bank for help, I was laughed at. In town, the kids would point me out as a fool. Nobody wanted to know me or your ma.'

Lisa listened as she followed him. Her ankle still hurt, although she rode while her father walked. Each jolting step sent a twinge of pain up her leg, and there was no way she could position the leg to ease the pain. When her father stopped once, to wipe sweat from his face and neck, she asked him, 'Why didn't you leave, Pa? Why didn't you take mother away if it was so hard, so useless?'

'Where else was there to go? Your ma needed a dry climate. Well, I sure enough gave her that. But it didn't matter in the end anyway. She died, slow and hard. It was then that I tried to sell out. But everybody I approached wasn't interested or at least said they weren't. I couldn't even get enough money together to get us south. So I just locked the door and took you down to your aunt. Then I came back to try again.'

Lisa saw his neck muscles tighten as his head lifted. His profile in the moonlight was that of a man hating everything about him.

He said, 'I found when I got back that a snivellin' jasper named Olsen, who'd been the one most against buying my place, had moved in. He'd run new fences, dug a well, and was running steers. After four years of drought, it'd rained. I went to him and asked him what was what, and four of his hired hands busted me up and threw me off the place.'

Lisa felt deep sympathy for her father, but she could find no words to console him.

Tom Moran talked on, 'Took me a week to walk again. I went looking for somebody to help me, but nobody wanted to even know me. So I did the only thing I could do.'

When her father was silent for a long time, Lisa asked, 'What was that, Pa?'

'I got a gun and I killed Olsen.'

Lisa gasped. Tom Moran looked at her, studying her gravely before he said, 'It was me against the whole bunch of 'em, and they had what was mine. So I killed that nester to show 'em. Then they hunted me. I was caught and thrown in a stinkin' jail and starved for a week. But my luck changed one night when the jailer was careless and I got his gun, knocked him out and escaped. For the next three years I was on the run. Then I met some men I could trust, and we started taking what we wanted, like everybody else was doing. In time, I got to be real fancy with a gun, one of the best, and men started to listen to me. I guess I started to live for the first time in my life. Things went real good and I sent you a lot of money and wrote often, because I had never had the chance to give you anything. A couple of times I visited you and we had some good times, but I kept my business away from you and your friends.'

'What are you saying, Pa? That you became an outlaw?'

'Sure I became an outlaw. I took what I wanted just like everybody else was doing. And if folks tried to stop me, it was just too bad for them.'

'You . . . you killed people?' she asked, shocked.

'When I had to. It was them or me, and I had to get something together for you. Then I ran into Lew Cavill. He had a burn in him against all my kind. He hunted me through this territory for nigh on four years before he caught up with me. He and his stinkin' deputy framed me for a lot of things I hadn't done, including the murder of three men in Sunfish Creek. But I'd made some friends in my time, and despite all their lies the judge sent me to prison for only two years. I hear he's since left the territory.'

Tom Moran chuckled to himself. 'He sure musta been scared to let me off so lightly, and he was even more scared when those scum started to beat his ears. But that's the breed a man has to put up with here – the judge, the sheriff and that damned deputy.'

Lisa felt sick. She could see now that there was no turning back unless she could convince her father that since he had served his time, he was now a free man. Nobody could make a charge against him now.

She said, 'Pa, listen to me. We've got to get off this mountain and go straight home. Aunt Bessie has saved most of your money and she wants me to buy a business for you. You can go back to your gunsmith trade.'

'My what?'

'Fixing guns, Pa. Uncle Jerome said—'

Moran's laughter drowned the rest of Lisa's words. 'So that's what the old buzzard told you about me, eh? Well, I guess at that he did me a favor. No, girl, I am what I am, and I have to do something before I think of settling down. I want you to understand that. This deputy will hunt me until one of us is dead. While he's alive, I won't be able to find peace anywhere. Every minute of every day I'll be watchin' for him to creep up.'

'But why, Pa? What have you done to him?'

'I did nothin' to him, girl. It's just the way he's made. From the beginning he was the driving force behind Cavill. He did the prompting and the pushing and the goading. He figured, I guess, that if he took care of me, then he'd be a big man. I was a name in his territory. Getting me would make him taller in everybody's eyes. But I beat him once, and ever since then he's made sure that I got word, weekly, that he was waiting for me to come out. That's why he penned up the Coolidge boys, to lure me into a trap. Maybe I'd have fallen for that trick, I don't know, but it shows you, don't it, just how far he's prepared to go?'

'But he can do nothing, Pa, nothing at all. Even if he caught up with you in the future, his hands would be tied.'

'His hands would hold a gun, Lisa,' Moran said. 'And that gun would be spitting death at me.' Moran shook his head and went on: 'No, it's Owen and Ed Coolidge and it doesn't matter who is first. Then maybe we'll start thinking about those plans of yours down south.'

Lisa held hard to the pommel of the saddle. Her body was quivering and she felt fatigue begin to take hold of her. Looking at her, Tom Moran was suddenly troubled.

'You all right, girl?'

Lisa didn't answer. She sat there, clinging to the saddle with all her strength, her eyes closed. Moran muttered a curse, stepped before the horse and walked on. He was almost out on his feet, but he paid no heed to his weariness. Ahead of him was Ed Coolidge, and Coolidge had double-crossed him and raped his daughter. Ed Coolidge had to be killed.

Blake Durant heard movement ahead and reined in. He slipped quietly out of the saddle and stroked Sundown gently. The big horse soon stood quiet, head down, resting.

Minutes passed before Blake heard the sound again. It was not far ahead of him. He hitched Sundown in light brush and drew his gun. Then he walked silently forward, making sure to steer clear of the brush stems and limbs of trees. For ten minutes he went on, stopping every few yards to listen again. The sounds of movement had stopped and there was nothing but the eerie singing of the night's silence.

Then suddenly he came onto a barren section. The light was bad, but it was sufficient to reveal a figure huddled against a rock. Blake leveled his gun and stepped forward. He recognized the sleeping man as Ed Coolidge when he was only two steps from him. Leaning over, he removed Coolidge's gun from its holster and tossed it into the brush. Ed Coolidge awakened with a start, only to look into the bore of Durant's gun.

Durant said, 'Trail's end for you, Coolidge.'

'Durant!'

The name was a hoarse cry from Coolidge. He flung his hand down for his gun but found the holster empty. He sat there, crushed, cursing Blake.

Blake went down on his haunches. He pushed the gun into Coolidge's face and said, 'I found the girl. What you did to her makes me want to shoot your face in. So sit and think about your future, mister. Think about rope.'

Coolidge's face jolted under sudden fear. 'I did nothin',' he called out. 'The girl's lyin'.'

'She didn't speak about it, Coolidge. She didn't have to. It was there in her face, the misery of a woman molested by an animal. You'll swing for that even if you don't hang for killing Sheriff Lew Cavill.'

'I didn't kill Cavill either, Durant,' Coolidge said angrily. 'That was Shelley. Hell, I didn't even have a gun.'

'You killed Gus Ivers,' Blake said.

'That old horse thief? He broke jail, too. Who's gonna hold that against me? And, anyway, it's your word against mine.'

Blake said, 'Owen will listen to me this time, Coolidge. But what I'm most worried about is

145

getting you past Tom Moran. Moran's gonna kill you when he catches up with you, and maybe I won't be able to stop him.'

Sweat glistened on Coolidge's drawn face. Blake decided he'd aged ten years since he was in the Sunfish Creek jailhouse. Blake settled down with the moonlight at his back, watching the light play over the face of the outlaw. He knew it was going to be a long night, but he was prepared for it. He had his man. The rest would be easy.

Or so he hoped.

TEN

THE TRAIL OUT

'I've got to rest, girl,' Tom Moran said to his daughter. 'I'm done in.'

Lisa felt the horse stop under her and then all her strength left her. She slipped from the saddle and staggered a few steps towards the brush. For an hour now they had had no difficulty in following the trail made by Blake Durant. But at no time had she caught a glimpse of him or the big black horse.

Sitting on the dead grass, she rubbed her swollen ankle. Her cuts and bruises and the welts on her face left there by Ed Coolidge's fists no longer worried her. In fact, nothing bothered her. Life had ceased to have meaning for her. For years now she had waited impatiently for the day when she would be with her father again. She had made so many plans to look after him and to make him settle down. But it didn't matter now. Whatever she had felt for her father was dead. He was a killer. He had murdered people to rob them. And that money he had taken he had sent home to her aunt. Lisa shuddered at the thought of the dresses she had so excitedly put on, dresses bought with an outlaw's money. She felt even worse than when Ed Coolidge had raped her.

'Be only half an hour at most, Lisa, then we'll push on. By the look of it, we should reach the foothills before morning. Then we'll talk some more.'

Lisa just sat there, numb. She did not know how much later it was that she heard her father stirring. He saddled the horse, gave it water from his canteen and then offered the canteen to her. Lisa accepted it, drank and handed it back. But when her father extended his hand to help her up, she turned away. She struggled into the saddle and let him lead her off, looking ahead at the gloomy terrain, praying for an end to it all.

For another hour they pressed on until Lisa heard a horse nicker. Her father stopped his mount on a barren stretch of ground and waved for her to be silent. Then Tom Moran walked on, leaving the horse with her. He found the big black stallion standing quietly between two boulders.

'Easy, boy,' he called softly, and Sundown shied away from his outstretched hand.

Then Blake Durant appeared only a few yards away. The big drifter said, 'Drop the gun, Moran.'

Moran whirled about, but he was in the moon-light while Durant's body was clothed in deep shadow. Moran knew he had no chance. He knew too that he would never make the mistake of underestimating this man again. Durant was smart and careful. He'd take a lot of handling.

Tom Moran put his gun back into its holster and said, 'You told me there was no burn between us, Durant. So why this?'

'Just a precaution, Moran,' Blake told him, then he stepped forward took the gun and called to Lisa to come on. The young woman wasted no time obeying his command. When they came to the small clearing, Lisa let out a gasp. Ed Coolidge was sitting on the far side of the clear-ing, glaring at her.

Tom Moran saw him at the same time. After a quick look at Durant, he asked, 'You gonna stop me goin' for him, Durant? Is that why you took my gun?'

Coolidge had his hands tied. He shifted awkwardly, trying to rise.

Durant said, 'Moran, I took your gun because I figure we've all walked far enough. Now we're going to sit. I think Billy Owen is close behind us and should find us by morning, that's if he or a member of his posse can read trail sign. Then we'll talk it out, I'll clear myself, and you can have the rest of it.'

Moran glared at him. 'I ain't waitin' for no damn sour-bellied deputy to come for me, Durant. I want Coolidge now. He rode with me, worked with me, drank with me. Then he raped my girl. You gonna stop a man takin' him apart when he's done that?'

'For now, Moran, just sit and be quiet. I think you've dragged your daughter too far too fast.'

Lisa looked gratefully at him, but Tom Moran was still in no mood to give in. Turning to Coolidge he said, 'It's gonna be slow, Ed, real slow. I'm gonna make you squirm and beg.'

Coolidge licked his lips and said nothing. Tom

Moran pulled the reins from Lisa's hands and pushed the horse to the edge of the clearing. He then sat down, legs crossed, and glared at Ed Coolidge.

'She's lyin', Tom,' Coolidge said a moment later. 'Hell, why would I want to do somethin' bad to her?'

'Because she's a woman, Ed. Not because she's a pretty woman, which she is, but because she's a woman. All the time I knew you, I watched you ogling women like an animal. You never had no woman of your own, because those you met couldn't stand the stink of you. The scum in you, Ed, smells high.'

Coolidge let out a groan and sank back against the rock. He lowered his eyes. His thigh hurt badly but he waited for a chance to run. He could run a hundred miles if only he could get away from here.

Blake Durant settled down on a patch of grass, keeping his gun on Coolidge. Lisa walked away from them and settled down on grass. Within minutes the place was quiet, Ed Coolidge's breathing the only disturbing noise.

Tom Moran made his move a long time later than

Blake Durant had expected him to. He went hurtling through the air, hands flailing when Blake Durant reached out for him. Moran let out a yell of pain and crashed heavily to the ground. Blake was over the top of him in two strides, imprisoning Moran's chest with his boots. He aimed his gun down at Moran's anger-filled face.

'I'll allow that one mistake, Moran. But there'll be no more or I'll tie you up. I don't know that it wouldn't be a good thing at that.'

Moran's face twisted. 'Go to hell, Durant. I can't sit there and listen to him snore. I've got to tear my hands at him. My girl—'

'Miss Moran doesn't need reminding about what happened, Moran. Sit and be quiet or so help me, I'll make you quiet.'

Blake stepped back but kept his gun trained on the outlaw. Tom Moran rose and glared at Ed Coolidge who looked away anxiously and then returned to his place. Lisa, who'd been sleeping, sat up and stroked her hair. But she didn't speak and her gaze rested only on Blake Durant.

Blake stretched out again. He wanted to catch some sleep, but doubted if he would during this long night. Again silence settled and it was quiet for two more hours – until the heavy trample of brush told them that Deputy Billy Owen and his posse had arrived.

Billy Owen halted at the head of his men and looked gravely about him. He had had no trouble following sign. So little trouble, in fact, that he was worried. He hadn't expected that it would be this easy.

Walsh drew up beside Owen and Bull Marner came after them. They sat their horses, all fatigued, as Walsh said, 'A short spell wouldn't hurt any, Deputy.'

Owen shook his head. 'No. We're close. I can feel it.'

'Only thing I can feel is my seat burnin',' put in Bull Marner. 'I ain't used to this, Owen.'

'Nobody's much used to it, mister, but you don't hear anybody else whinin', do you?'

'Maybe the others ain't got the energy left to whine, mister,' Marner answered gruffly. 'We gonna rest or not? I feel like this whole mountain has been hammering at me.'

Owen thought of Durant and Ed Coolidge. He was still supremely confident that he could handle the issue on his own. But there was the woman. He needed somebody to look after her.

Getting her killed through a rash move wouldn't do much to get the respect he craved. He had seen disrespect in their eyes.

'Ten minutes then,' Owen said. 'I suggest that you walk about and stretch your legs.'

Nobody argued with him. But Owen sat on his horse, watching the first gray light of day begin to creep along the side of the mountain. Suddenly he was tense again, waving wildly at Walsh and Marner and another couple of men still pacing back and forth through the brush.

'Hush down,' he ordered, and the four men stopped. The others, yards away, followed their example until the whole area was quiet.

'What is it?' asked Walsh.

'Can't you smell it, mister?' Owen said.

Walsh lifted his head a fraction and sniffed. 'I don't smell nothin'.'

But Bull Marner soon put in, 'A fire. Yeah, I can smell somethin' burnin'.'

'They likely figure they got away from us,' Owen said. 'But they didn't. We've got 'em. By hell, we've got 'em.'

'We ain't got nobody yet,' Walsh said. 'Work it out proper, Deputy. None of us is going blind into something we ain't sure about.'

'But you're going in, mister, because you're sworn in and there are killers down there not far from us. If you don't, mister, the whole town is gonna hear about the way your guts crawled at the thought of facing outlaws.'

Still grinning, Billy Owen slipped from the saddle. He quickly organized the horses into a huddle in thick brush and left one man to look after them. Then he called his posse together and said, 'Marner and two others, get down the trail a little more and position yourselves past the fire. You'll see it soon enough. Walsh can stay here and come down that passage between them two boulders. The rest of you come with me and do what I tell you.'

Owen pushed Marner down the trail. Two men followed the big man. As soon as they'd gone from sight, Owen pointed out the faint light of a fire no more than thirty yards from them. Breathing in deeply, he drew his gun and led the three men forward. It took him only a few minutes to reach the edge of the clearing where he could see the fire burning clearly. But the clearing was empty except for two horses, one the big black belonging to Blake Durant.

Owen stood there, his companions backed up

behind him. He said, 'We'll surround the place. Keep out of sight until you see somebody. Then call to them to stay put. If it's Durant or Coolidge, shoot them down.'

The men exchanged worried glances. Like Walsh and Marner, they had decided that Blake Durant's actions did not point him out to be anything but an innocent man. But they also knew it would do no good arguing that point with Owen.

They moved off while the tall deputy stood, gun in hand, his heart beating hard. He'd been alone for barely a minute when he felt something press against his spine. Then came Blake Durant's voice:

'Just walk forward, Deputy, and don't try to best me.'

Owen jerked his head about. 'Durant, damn you, I'll—'

'The first thing you'll do, mister, is call out to your men. I want them bunched where I can see them, doing nothing till they hear me out.'

'Go to hell, drifter!'

'If you don't, Owen, you're going to force me to hit you again as I had to do in town. Walk, damn you!'

Blake pushed the deputy into the ring of light

coming from the small fire. It was only then that Owen saw the three huddled forms in the cover of brush on the other side of the small clearing. Owen halted just short of the fire, glaring at Durant. Then, without being asked, Walsh, Marner and the rest of the posse showed themselves.

Blake understood immediately by the nods of greeting from the posse men that they meant him no harm. He took Owen's gun and tossed it aside, then he walked to where Ed Coolidge was looking fearfully up at him.

Blake pointed to him and said, 'You all know this man. He killed Gus Ivers when we caught up with him at the shack. That's enough for you to hang him for, if not for the killing of your sheriff. I hunted him down for the simple reason that bringing him back for trial would show you all that I had no hand in any of Tom Moran's business or in the killing of your sheriff.'

Blake then pointed to Tom Moran. 'I guess you all know Moran. I don't give a damn what you want with him, but from what I've learned he's got a burn to get revenge for what he considers to be injustice. And I don't give a damn about that. But the girl is his daughter and she's suffered badly during this manhunt, so treat her right.'

Blake looked keenly at Owen. 'Mister, you're not fit to wear tin. You're walking too tall and wanting too much. Keep it up and you'll walk into trouble too big for you to handle.'

Blake then walked across to Tom Moran and cut him loose. Moran stood rubbing his hands together to get the circulation back in them. Blake was helping Lisa to her feet when Moran suddenly grabbed her and wheeled her about, lifting her off the ground so that her ankles struck Blake in the chest and sent him reeling. Billy Owen charged forward but Moran hurled his daughter at the deputy and then grabbed one of the posse men. With a savage twist of the man's arm he disarmed him and scooped up the fallen gun. Ed Coolidge let out a loud howl of fear as Tom Moran swung back and glared at him.

'Ed, you shouldn't've done it.'

Moran pumped three shots into Ed Coolidge who gave no more than a grunt before he collapsed. Billy Owen lunged over the fire. Tom Moran swung back to meet his challenge and his teeth peeled back in a savage snarl as he pumped two shots into him. Owen staggered into the fire and then past it. Then he fell and lay still, the flames licking at his hands.

Lisa Moran's scream was drowned by sudden firing from Walsh and Bull Marner. Their bullets thudded into a retreating Tom Moran and sent him crashing back into the brush. Lisa let out another scream as Blake Durant, back on his feet, looked about him.

Ed Coolidge. Tom Moran. Deputy Billy Owen. All dead. He looked thoughtfully at the other men and crossed to Lisa Moran. Without a word, he lifted her into the saddle, and then he faced the posse.

'You men got anything against me?'

Walsh shook his head and extended his hand. 'If you ever come through Sunfish Creek again, Durant, try my saloon. You'll find it more hospitable than the jailhouse.'

Blake nodded. Lisa was looking to where her father had fallen in the brush, knowing he was dead.

Blake said, 'They'll bury him.'

Lisa nodded.

'You don't want to stay here?' he asked.

Lisa shook her head. Then she bit her lip, lowered her head and Blake could hear her sobbing as he got onto Sundown and rode off.

Daylight had come.

In half an hour they were on the prairie and heading south. Lisa had told him on the way that her ankle hurt and she wanted to go home. She begged him to stay with her. Blake Durant had given her no argument. He was again on a trail to nowhere, his painful memories forgotten for the moment. He was with a girl who had guts and spirit. He wondered how it would end.